Imperfect Acts

Also by Peter Shianna

Take Off
Love Tag
Flawed Justice

Imperfect Acts

Peter Shianna

The Red Oak Readers Press
Lady Lake, Florida

ISBN-13: 978-0615923277 / ISBN-10: 0615923275

The Red Oak Readers Press
P.O. Box 2155
Lady Lake, FL 32158-2155

Cover Design by Peter Shianna
Cover Art by Charlene Meeker
Cover by Jerry Hicks, Ultrex Printing

For Lori

ACKNOWLEDGEMENTS

Huge thanks to Shawn Shianna, who provided a wealth of insights and suggestions way back when this work entered the world as a screen play.

My gratitude to Marsha Butler, Sarah Nell Summers, and Joan West for their invaluable editing and overall input.

Thank you Mary Lois Sanders for your support and wonderful technical expertise.

Last but far from least, thank you Lori for enduring this seemingly never-ending quest.

Also

The author expresses his appreciation to Alfred Publishing Company, Inc. for permission to print the lyrics of "Somewhere My Love" by Paul Francis Webster, music by Maurice Jarre.

"He [Judge Max Rosenn, U.S. Third Circuit Court of Appeals] taught me not to seek the truth, but the truth of the case."

Rick Matasar, Iowa College of Law, quoted by Mollie Marti, JD, PhD, in *Walking with Justice*.

PART I

Chapter One
1986

Roger Walker had once read that danger doesn't build character but reveals it. He brushed his sweaty hands across his jeans and stepped onto the loading dock that jutted out from the shipping room.

"Yo, Virgil," he called to a man near a pale blue pickup.

Virgil Badeen twisted around.

Roger bent down to brace himself on his left hand as he swung off the concrete loading dock and landed with a jolt on the asphalt parking lot. "What's that you're putting in your truck?"

Badeen glanced down at the ax in his hands and rolled the handle a half-turn. "Just a ax, Roger. What're you doing back here?"

Roger stopped two paces from Badeen. "Stealing ain't right. I know it and so do you."

Surrounded by a neatly trimmed, close-cropped beard, Badeen's little-boy grin vanished and reappeared an instant before he spoke. "Come on, Roger. We're friends, ain't we? No sense us getting crossways."

The shift had ended, but the four o'clock sun stayed on the clock. Roger resisted the urge to wipe away a trickle of sweat running down his face along his right ear. He had to walk a thin line with Badeen.

"All I'm saying is, it's wrong to take another man's property."

"What man?"

"Man or company, makes no difference."

"I suppose you know about that, being a part-time preacher and all. I believe in the Good Book too. Who says

3

this ain't my own ax?"

Roger nudged his glasses higher on his nose. Scuffing at the soft asphalt with the sole of his boot, he wondered how hot it was. The thermometer hit ninety-two at three o'clock, still had to be close to that. Way too warm for this early in spring, and humid enough to shave without lather.

"Your own ax have LaFarge Paper burned into it? I saw the handle before you flipped it."

Badeen's grin disappeared. "Maybe you saw wrong." The grin returned. "Had them glasses checked lately?"

Roger leaned forward and reached for the ax. Badeen pivoted away, his right hand on the ax handle next to the blade, his left hand holding the other end. The ax handle pressed against a gray vinyl pouch attached to his belt.

"Don't do that, Roger! Ain't my word good enough?"

Roger backed away, not sure what to do next. Badeen's arms were massive, larger than Roger's legs.

"Don't charity begin at home, Roger? You know my momma's crippled up. I've got to lay in firewood for her and me both." Badeen's eyes bored through the space between himself and Roger. "You know how long she's been in that wheel chair? They let me out so's I could take care of her."

"I'm sorry about your mother. I know you take care of her, and I respect that. Why don't you go buy yourself your own ax?"

Badeen's face flushed and quivered. His chest heaved with every breath. He shifted farther to his right and slid his right hand along the ax handle until it met his left, like a baseball player gripping a bat.

Roger clenched his jaws. A tingling sensation shot through his teeth. Why'd he confront Badeen? Only a damn fool would do this. But he'd had enough of the man. Everybody in the plant feared the jerk and wouldn't stand up to him. No going back now.

He would try to evade the blow if Badeen swung the ax. If he couldn't dodge the blade, he hoped the ax would catch him square and fatal, not glance off his head or slash his collarbone or ribs.

"I like you, Roger. You ain't like the rest. Don't make me do this. I won't go back there, and I don't want to get fired. You know, my momma and all?"

"I ain't making you do nothing. If you do it, you do it because you want to. Plain and simple." He thumbed his glasses higher on his nose again.

Badeen swayed from left to right like a batter waiting for a slow-working pitcher to deliver, his blue eyes never losing their hold on Roger's, his long blond hair rippling as he swayed.

Streaks of sweat streamed down Roger's face. He squinted against the sun, his stomach burned. "You give me the ax, I won't say nothing to nobody. You won't get fired."

Not a drop of sweat showed on Badeen's face. He stopped swaying.

"Virgil, you know I can't let you take company property, even if you kill me. You have to respect that."

Badeen swiped a forearm over his stubbled baby-face. His breathing audible, he shifted his weight to his back foot and tightened his grip on the ax.

His eyes burrowed into Roger again.

Roger tensed and held his breath.

The ax swung low over the ground like a pendulum as Badeen revolved in a slow circle on the asphalt. A sound between a moan and a whine escaped his pursed lips. He faced Roger and tilted his head skyward with closed eyes.

"Momma," he said mostly to himself, "forgive Virgie, I know you will, Momma. I don't know why people make me do things, I really don't, and you know I don't want nothing bad for you, things just get all mixed up." Muscles in his huge arms flexed. Veins bulged against his fair skin.

The ax pendulum swung higher. Roger swallowed hard against the tightness in his throat. Should he break and run? No. *Thou art my strength. Thy will be done.*

Badeen's eyes remained closed. His blond locks slow-danced while his arms and body swayed with the ax. He stopped. The ax stopped. He opened his eyes and glared at Roger. "I thought you was different."

Roger returned Badeen's stare while keeping the ax blade at the edge of his sight.

The ax came up, though not the way Roger expected. Badeen extended the ax outward parallel with the ground. "You take it, Roger." The grin flashed. "You're a good man."

Roger grasped the handle with both hands. Badeen didn't let go. They stood on the baked asphalt like mannequins, their eyes locked on each other. Roger needed to swallow the dryness at the top of his throat, but he didn't want Badeen to see him do it, *couldn't* let him see it.

Without warning, Badeen released his grip and stepped back. Wheeling around, he climbed into his pickup.

The engine fired. The truck crept across the parking lot to the stop sign at the county road where it remained for several seconds before ripping forward. Smoke and the stench of burning rubber spewed into the parched air. The vehicle careened down the road and disappeared behind a stand of chalk maples at the property line of LaFarge Paper Company.

The heat continued to suck oxygen from the air as Roger returned to the loading dock. The odor of chlorine and other chemicals from inside the plant mingled with the heat and poured into his lungs with a mild corrosive sensation. A touch of breeze fluttered through his sweat-soaked shirt. When he tried to clear his throat, everything in his stomach surged up instead.

Dropping the ax, he stretched both arms forward to the edge of the dock, leaned over, and retched a foul mess that burned his throat. Dry heaves seared his chest. Lightheaded and shaky, he spit residue until most of the vile taste went away. He wiped his mouth with a limp blue handkerchief from his back pocket.

He had done right and felt something. Not bravery, but something. The ax handle was moist when he picked it up. He wiped his hands on his pants and hoped for no more trouble with Badeen.

Chapter Two

Jason Ferris drove the shovel into the soft earth with a thrust of his right leg. He turned the clump of soil over and sliced it into smaller clumps with the tip of the shovel, his lean body glistening with sweat in the warm sunshine.

Inhaling the fresh spring air, he stood straight and leaned on the shovel. Luke, a brown, medium-size short-hair dog of vague ancestry and conspicuous ears, lay on the grass alongside the garden. A robin tugged a reluctant worm from the moist earth as wrens twittered nearby. Jason glanced at his watch, frowned, and turned the soil with renewed vigor.

"Hi, Jason!" Cari Lang strode across the lawn from next door carrying a yellow plastic mug. Her orange cutoff T-shirt ended above her navel well north of her low-cut white shorts. The dog rolled to his feet and loped toward her.

"Hiya, Luke! How you doing?" She reached down to scratch the dog's ears before she handed the mug to Jason.

"Lemonade? Thanks!"

"Want to go biking when you get done?"

"Nope. My dad's taking me fishing when he gets off work. Walleyes're biting like crazy in the Rock River."

"Fishing. Don't you ever think of anything else?"

"Sure. Camping."

"Oooo! How different! Live wild, Ferris!"

Laughing and choking on the lemonade, Jason tilted toward Cari and squirted a stream of lemonade at her bare feet.

She danced away. "Gross!"

"That's for a smartass sophomore."

"From a *very* juvenile freshman!"

Jason laughed again, drank the lemonade in two gulps,

and handed the empty mug back to Cari. "Thanks. That really hit the spot. I'd better get back to work." When Cari didn't answer, Jason followed her gaze across the county road to where Clem Ferguson worked bare-headed at a beehive, one of a dozen or so a hundred yards beyond the road.

Cari shook her head. "I wouldn't do that for anything."

"Heck, they don't sting unless they get riled up. Mr. Ferguson taught me all about bees. Lets me help sometimes. He knows a lot about bees. I might raise them myself someday."

"Haven't you heard about killer bees? Like taking over the whole country?"

"Come on, Cari. These are just plain old honeybees. They don't hurt anybody."

Cari shivered and grimaced. "Creepy. Want to go biking tomorrow?"

"Sure."

"Oh, I almost forgot." She reached into the pocket of her tight shorts and pulled out a medallion-size brass violin. She handed it to him.

"For me? Gosh, thanks!" He examined it closely.

"Do you like it?"

"Sure do!"

"I'm glad. Well, I have to go practice."

She glided away, her firm, shapely butt jiggling just enough and her long, tanned legs going up and up and up. Jason watched until she reached her back steps and turned to wave at him. He waved back and closed his eyes for as long as it took him to inhale and hold a deep breath.

Biting his lip, he stabbed the shovel into the damp earth. The work had to get done if he wanted to go fishing with his dad. Besides, turning the soil would help quell the agonizing excitement in his jeans.

Minutes later, his dad's weathered red pickup turned off the county road. The truck made a U-turn on the gravel driveway, backed up, and stopped inches short of an aluminum boat on a rusty trailer next to the garage.

Jason ran over to hitch the trailer to the pickup. Mike

Ferris emerged from the truck carrying a blue and white vinyl lunch bucket. Splotches of sweat covered most of his blue shirt and darkened the rim of his tan and white LaFarge Paper Company cap.

"Got that garden done?"

"Almost."

"Finish her off. Soon as we eat, we're out of here."

Jason stood in the boat casting toward a weed bed close to shore. Nothing in the world could beat fishing, just the two of them, on a day like this. He wished it would stay daylight until tomorrow. He knew his dad enjoyed it too.

Perched on the seat closest to the outboard motor, his dad laid his rod down and leaned back against the motor housing. "Time to pack it in, son. We've got four nice ones for the freezer. That's enough for today."

"Just a few more casts?"

"Okay. I'll have another shot of Kool-Aid. Bet I drink more of this stuff than anybody. They should hire me for a commercial. Kool Mike Ferris, famous actor." He laughed, poured lime Kool-Aid into the Thermos lid, and gulped a swallow. Shadows had sneaked over the bank of the small inlet they had found, the air had cooled, and wavelets lapped against the boat. "When it's like this, I could stay out here forever."

"Me too, Dad."

"Garden of Eden couldn't a been more peaceful."

"Think Mom will ever come with us again?" He had more fun when only the two of them fished together, but he had almost as much fun when his mom joined them. She liked to fish and always packed good snacks.

"Might help her headaches, daggone things."

Jason flipped his lure next to the weeds and water lilies near shore. When his mom fished with them, she lightened up and seemed to enjoy herself.

"Why does she worry so much about everything, Dad?"

His dad took a sip of Kool-Aid and didn't answer right away. Jason kept casting.

"Her last confine … her last stay was rough on her. Long as she takes her medication, she should be okay. You and me got to cut her plenty of slack, understand?"

"You bet, Dad."

Night had fallen by the time they got home. Linda met them at the door.

"I thought you both had drowned and we'd have to drag the river bottom for you. Can't you get enough fishing during daylight?" She always got a little cross when they stayed out late.

Jason's dad winked at him. "Those daggone fish kept jumping in the boat. We tried to leave a long time ago, but every time we got close to shore we had another load of fish to throw back."

"Tell me another one, Ferris." She couldn't help smiling. "By the way, Cari dropped this off for you," she said to Jason, handing him a folded sheet of music.

"Thanks, Mom!"

He took the music to his room, where he read the lyrics of "Somewhere, My Love."

> *Somewhere, my love, there will be songs to sing*
> *Although the snow covers the hopes of spring*
> *Somewhere a hill blossoms in green and gold*
> *And there are dreams, all that your heart can hold*
> *Someday we'll meet again, my love*
> *Someday whenever the spring breaks through*
>
> *You'll come to me out of the long-ago*
> *Warm as the wind, soft as the kiss of snow*
> *Till then, my sweet, think of me now and then*
> *Godspeed, my love, till you are mine again!*

He decided to go see Cari as soon as he cleaned up and got rid of the fish smell. How could he think of anything else after reading those lyrics?

Chapter Three

Jason and Cari took turns keeping the swing in motion with foot nudges against the floor. Jason loved this time of evening. The sawing of crickets and rasping of tree frogs mingled with the squeaking of the swing on the Lang front porch. The heat of day had surrendered to evening, the air felt and smelled cool, and the subdued sounds of night even made the darkness *sound* cool. Cool and fresh and mysterious.

The jumpy flickering and muffled voices from a television in the living room flashed into the night through the screen door and ricocheted off the trees.

Unmindful of the cacophony surrounding him, Luke lay sprawled out on the floor near the swing. Cari cradled a violin on her lap.

"Not only her medicine," Jason said. "She eats aspirin like candy and worries all the time."

Cari set the violin on the floor next to Luke. She touched Jason's hand.

The feel of her hand kick-started his heart and made his breathing shallow.

"You have to stay positive."

"Maybe you're right." His voice felt breathy.

She leaned against him. "Do you really like the lyrics to 'Somewhere, My Love,' or did you just say that to be nice?"

"Darn right I meant it. The words are beautiful." Catching the pleased look on her face, he added, "Too bad your violin is so squawky."

She punched him on the shoulder. "You know you like my music."

"I've gotten used to it. Like a toothache, you know?"

Cari stroked his arm, leaning closer. "Ever ... you know."

"What?"

"You know."

"What?"

"Kissed a girl?"

"Sure."

"I mean a real kiss? Like they do it in the movies?"

Jason peered into the darkness where fireflies winked their mating codes. Could he trust his voice? What should he say?

"Well, no, I guess not."

"Ever thought about it?"

"Yeah. Sure." He hoped he sounded cool.

Cari gazed at him expectantly.

Jason's eyes met hers. She was so pretty, the prettiest girl he knew or could imagine. And fun, too. She excited him above his shoulders and below his belt, two sensations he loved but worried about.

"I'd better not."

Cari leaned away. "Jeez, Ferris, you can kiss a girl and still be a priest someday."

"I don't think it's, like, such a good idea. You know?"

Cari pushed her feet hard against the floor. The swing squeaked and lurched backward. Luke raised his head.

"It's not like we're going to *do* it or anything," she said.

"Maybe we should lighten up."

Her crossed arms told him he had hurt her feelings. "I'm sorry," he said.

"Maybe you should just go home. Maybe you'd rather be alone."

Jason glanced at Luke. "Maybe you're right."

"Don't be so literal, Ferris!"

Luke raised his head, then flopped back down as soon as Cari reached down and scratched his ears.

"Why do you want to be a priest, anyway?"

"Like you don't know?"

"Is a promise to your mom when you're ten like a contract or something? Bet your mom doesn't think so."

"I believe my mom and God want me to be a priest."

"I believe God wants us to have some fun."

"Fun things can go wrong. That's why confession is so important. When I do something wrong, I can't wait to get to confession."

"Jeez Louise, Ferris! You trying to convert me or what? Methodists don't have confession, remember?"

Luke rolled onto his belly.

"Gosh, Cari, don't get goofy. I just don't want to do anything I'll regret afterwards."

"Just go home and take your sermon with you!"

She slid off the swing, snatched her violin, and marched into the house. The screen door clacked against the frame behind her.

Frightened, Luke half-climbed onto Jason's lap. Jason scratched the dog's ears. "It's okay, boy, it's okay. Don't be afraid."

He eased Luke down and got off the swing. "Let's go home."

They headed across the dark spongy lawn. Midway, Jason knelt on the grass and threw his arms around Luke.

"Women!"

Chapter Four

Mike Ferris's stomach had begun nagging in a whisper an hour ago. Now it screamed. He tugged back the cuff of his shirt to expose his watch: Five minutes to noon. LaFarge Paper could afford five minutes extra for lunch on a Friday. He parked the lift truck next to a flatbed semi opposite the loading dock and grabbed his lunch box from behind the seat.

He decided to eat outside rather than in the air-conditioned cafeteria. Who needed air-conditioning on a nice spring day like this?

The cafeteria offered grilled sandwiches, soups, and salads at low prices that were a good deal in the winter or when temperatures soared in the summer. Most workers usually brought their own lunches and ate them in the cafeteria or outside.

Mike liked what Linda packed for him, except every so often when she slipped in a couple of god-awful tuna salad sandwiches. Whenever she did that, he had the urge to drive home and give them to Luke. Good thing she did it only once or twice a year, probably because she was out of other stuff. No sense making her feel bad by complaining. She knew what he liked and didn't like.

Mike headed for the LaFarge Hilton, the name someone had given to a small grove of cottonwood trees behind the plant where the company had built some permanent park tables and benches on concrete slabs. The trees offered shade and a place to smoke, which wasn't allowed inside the plant.

Seven men already had gathered at the tables. Roger Pell, the fat union steward, sat at one table with two others, including the foreman, Roger Walker. Virgil Badeen and three other workers sat together at the next table. Mike liked Walker and Pell, so he joined them.

He opened his lunch box to find two ham and cheese sandwiches nestled between a cup of vanilla yogurt, an apple, and a bag of chips. A thermos of cold milk would round out an excellent lunch. A nice ripple of air felt good across his sweaty forehead.

"As I was saying," Roger said, "Mr. Davis said the numbers for the second quarter look as good as the first quarter, maybe better. Good news for our profit sharing."

Everyone at the table nodded.

"Company keeps most of the profit," Badeen said from the next table.

Roger finished his bite of sandwich and sipped his coffee. "Well, yeah, maybe so, but we get a good hunk. It adds up. Someday my baby girl will go to college with that money, and I'll retire on it."

"Company keeps most of it."

Mike saw Roger's predicament. He didn't want an argument with hothead Badeen, but he didn't want to back down in front of the men either. Nobody else said a word.

"Maybe you're right, Virgil. I don't know all the ins and outs. I'm just glad we have a good profit sharing plan."

"Who says it's good? This outfit screws us over every chance it gets."

A stillness fell over the group of men. Even the breeze seemed to have gone off somewhere to rest.

"Hell, Virgil, they pay better than anyone else around here. Good benefits, too. No place is perfect."

Mike waved a fly away from his yogurt and slid a little to his right on the bench into a shady spot. Roger had it right. LaFarge Paper had a waiting list of people who wanted a job. Why didn't Badeen shut up? He'd been a troublemaker from day one.

"Blood money," Badeen said. "And why are you swearing? Preachers ain't supposed to swear. Even part-timers."

A tad of color came into Roger's face. He took another sip of coffee. "It's a free country. We can all have our opinion.

You're right, though. I shouldn't cuss."

"I've had enough of your preaching."

No one moved. It was quiet as a cemetery.

With a glance at his watch, Roger gathered up what remained of his lunch and pushed himself up from the table.

"If the pay is so good, Mr. Foreman, why do you drive that rattletrap piece of junk you call a car?"

Roger's face flushed. Mike ground his teeth and wished he'd gone to the cafeteria. He knew Roger donated heavily to his church and, sure, the man was frugal to a fault and took a lot of kidding for it. Now, in front of the men, Badeen's remark had embarrassed him. Roger started to walk away.

"Words are cheap preacher man. Are you a phony in the pulpit, too?"

Roger halted. He turned slowly to face Badeen. "How much did your last job pay, Virgil?"

The look on Badeen's face turned dark. Everyone knew he'd been in prison before the LaFarge family gave him a chance at a good job.

Mike's stomach roiled as Badeen rose from the bench. God Almighty, he was a mountain of muscle.

Badeen just stood there staring at Roger. Then he advanced toward him until his chest was only inches from Roger's face. His icy blue eyes bored into the smaller man's for maybe ten seconds, though it seemed like ten minutes. Badeen smiled. No, it wasn't a smile, or even what you could call a smirk. Whatever it was, Mike knew he would never forget the look on Badeen's face.

Only the shrieking of a blue jay overhead broke the silence as Badeen turned and swaggered off.

Roger cleared his throat. "Okay, everybody. Let's get back to work."

Glad the lunch break had ended, Mike's heart downshifted to normal. He didn't like Virgil Badeen and wished he'd never been hired. Why couldn't the jerk learn to get along with people? Target shooting with Jason after work would be a welcome relief.

Chapter Five

Jason fidgeted in his chair and watched his dad squirt ketchup on his last hot dog. He could sure take his time when he wanted to. Jason had finished eating five minutes ago. His mom had finished before that. She never ate enough to weigh down a hummingbird in the first place.

He wasn't supposed to begin clearing dishes until his parents had eaten the last of their meal. Jason couldn't wait. He pushed his chair back and said, "I'd better get this plate rinsed off."

He gathered his plate, utensils, and water glass, and headed for the sink while his dad ate his final hot dog and drained the lime Kool-Aid from his glass.

"Guns're in the truck, Dad."

His dad smiled and tugged on his mustache. He winked at Linda. "Let's load up the dishwasher first. These dishes ain't gonna clean theirself."

Frowning, Jason began collecting the dishes.

"You two get going," Linda said. "I'll clear the table. Just be sure you're back in time to clean the garage. You said you'd do that a month ago."

Mike embraced her playfully. "We can't hardly wait to clean out that old garage. What's a Friday afternoon for, anyway?" Behind Linda's back he squinted his eyes and stuck out his tongue at Jason, who smothered a laugh.

A minute later they piled into the old Ford pickup.

"Think you can hit anything today?" his dad asked.

"You watch. Won't be a can standing when I'm done."

His dad laughed and stepped on the gas.

They carried a black plastic garbage bag full of aluminum

cans into the played out gravel pit. Jason set the cans on ledges and outcroppings of the old pit while his dad loaded the guns.

"Let's see what you can do," his dad said, handing Jason a Colt .22 revolver. Jason took aim, squeezed the trigger, and missed. He fired four more times and hit two cans. His misses were close.

"Not bad. Not bad at all. Load her up."

Jason reloaded the .22, leaving one chamber empty, just like his dad had taught him.

"Let me have a go," his dad said. He fired five times in rapid succession and sent five cans spinning. He laid the .22 on a rock. Sliding a black nine-millimeter pistol from the holster on his hip, he took aim at a can and squeezed the trigger. Compared to the .22, the nine-millimeter sounded like a cannon going off. The bullet ripped the can.

"Okay, son. Show me your stuff with the nine." He handed the pistol to Jason. "You know how the safety works?"

"Sure do."

"Always operate the safety with your finger off the trigger and wrapped around the trigger guard. You don't want the weapon slipping around in your hand, and you don't want your finger on the trigger."

"Right."

Jason gripped the pistol and scanned the remaining targets.

"Lock your wrist and aim low. Use both hands like I told you. Which one you going for?"

"Bud Light can on the left."

The pistol bellowed and kicked skyward. The soft-nose bullet blasted against the rocks three feet above the beer can.

"Aim lower and squeeeeeze. What's your hurry? You got a date with a super model?"

The next shot missed by only inches.

"Don't flinch. It ain't a rattlesnake, it ain't a black widow, and it ain't gonna bite."

Jason's third shot barely missed. The fourth sent the shredded can spinning into the air.

"There you go! That's how you do it!"

They high-fived each other and began reloading. They shot up three boxes of .22 shells and a box of the nine-millimeters. By the time they finished and collected the cans for recycling, Jason had begun hitting nearly every target.

Later, his dad parked on the driveway and eased out of the pickup. "Check those guns again to make sure they're empty and leave them in the truck for now. I'll start on the garage."

When Jason caught up, he found his dad standing hands on hips next to an Everlast speed bag that dangled from a plywood platform. His dad poked the scruffy bag with his left fist. "You been working this bag?"

"Yep."

"Show me."

Jason reached for a pair of training gloves looped over a nail on the wall, tugged them on, and began: jab, backhand, jab, backhand, jab, hard right, for about twenty blows before missing and sending the bag a kilter.

"Pretty good. Here, give me the gloves."

His dad yanked on the gloves and worked the bag over with both hands like a pro. At least three times faster than Jason's punching, and with a smooth tempo, he backhanded with hard, effortless beauty and never missed a rebound.

He stilled the bag by clasping it between his hands.

"Let's try the big gloves for a round," he said to Jason.

"You must want to get knocked out."

His dad smiled and tugged at his mustache. "Wouldn't be the first time."

They lifted two pairs of old scuffed boxing gloves from another nail, pulled them on, and circled each other with gloves held high. Mike grazed Jason's cheek with a jab, then feinted and hit Jason lightly on the jaw.

"Don't counter like that with your right when I jab. Use your left."

"Okay, Dad."

His dad blocked and slipped Jason's punches while landing his own at will, not hard at first, but as they continued he began to pop Jason a little harder. Jason danced away. He scraped a glove across his face and gulped for air. His dad threw a left jab and right cross combination. Jason bobbed, ducked to his right, and doubled his dad over with a hard right uppercut to the belly, then a left jab that caught his chin, followed by a stiff right to the nose. His dad's eyes flashed; he began to counter but backed off instead, laughing.

"That's how to do it! Let's clean this garage before you beat me up too bad."

They cradled the gloves on the nail. His dad turned away from him, but not before he saw the trickle of blood from his dad's nose. Jason started to say something but stopped. He hated the sight of blood, his own or anyone else's. His dad wasn't really hurt, no big deal or anything. Just the same he felt sick to his stomach and knew he never wanted to box with his dad again.

Chapter Six

Mike parked the forklift next to concrete steps that led to the door of the pulp room. He climbed off the machine, bounded up the steps to the steel door, slipped off his sunglasses, and slid them into his shirt pocket. The door wouldn't budge when he tried to open it. He tried again with the same result. With the heel of his hand, he pounded on the door and waited before pounding a second time.

"Open up! Why's the daggone door locked?"

The door cracked open, then opened wide. An arm shot out and grabbed Mike's shirt at the chest and yanked him inside. The door slammed shut. Billy Sinkhorn rammed the bolt of the lock across the frame. He gripped Mike's arm and shoved him forward until he stood next to Marvin Pell, the fat union steward. Mike's eyes began to adjust to the indoor light, his nose to the smell of chlorine and hydrogen peroxide.

"No one else."

Mike followed the voice to a steel platform next to a large pulp tank where Virgil Badeen stood with one arm around Roger Walker's neck and the other twisting Roger's arm behind his back.

"What in hell's going on?" Mike said.

"Shut up, Ferris!" Badeen said. "I wanted Marvin here. Didn't count on no one else."

Sinkhorn released Mike's arm and climbed the steps to join Badeen on the platform. Mike noticed the large steel pulley chained to Roger's leg.

"We all know our preacher-man foreman is a spy," Badeen said. "Remember Ellis? Got fired for taking a winch from the yard. You tell the manager, Roger?" He twisted Roger's arm until he grimaced. Tears trickled down his face.

"Anything goes on in this plant, management knows right off. You know how much I hate to do this, Roger? Makes me sad. Real sad. But you're making me do it. It's your fault. I need to protect myself and every other worker in this here plant." He wrenched Roger's arm hard. Roger cried out in pain.

"Now I need me a new ax so's I can heat my house and my momma's house. How would you like being in a wheelchair in the dead of winter with no heat? You know how cold it gets around here? What's a twenty-dollar ax to a twenty-million dollar company?"

Mike's stomach churned. *You've scared him enough. Let the poor man go.* The thought struck him: Maybe they intend to do more than scare him. *Jesus!*

A hard punch to Roger's belly doubled him over. Badeen yanked him upright and glared at Marvin Pell below. "Pay attention, steward. We don't need this spy around, and I don't want the union or the company messing with me. Got that?"

Pell swallowed and nodded. Badeen slapped Roger and jammed him against a steel girder. A despairing moan rose from deep within the poor man.

"He knows what's coming. Me and Billy told him, so's he could suffer real good in his head first."

"Please don't, Virgil! I won't say anything! I promise!"

"Too late, preacher."

Mike stepped forward. "You've scared him enough. Let him go."

Badeen glared at Mike in a way that left no room for more talk. "One word about this from you or Pell and you're both dead. First your families, then you. Don't mess with me and Billy and my brother. I'm a boy scout next to my brother."

"Virgil, I've got a wife and kid! I'll never say a word! Please don't do this!" Roger's voice had become a high-pitched wail.

"Pick up the pulley, Billy."

"No! No! Dear God, help me! Somebody help me!"

Roger babbled and cried hysterically as Badeen lifted him off the platform. Sinkhorn picked up the pulley. Kicking and twisting and screaming, Roger was no match for Badeen, but one wild kick caught Sinkhorn in the groin. Sinkhorn gasped and dropped the pulley. Badeen held Roger in a bear hug to keep his arms pinned while Roger's free leg thrashed wildly. His glasses flew off his face.

Sinkhorn retrieved the pulley and three feet of slack chain that attached the pulley to Roger's leg. Avoiding the man's kicks, Sinkhorn hammered the pulley as hard as he could against Roger's knee. The cracking sound told Mike the blow had broken the knee. Roger screamed and stopped kicking long enough for Sinkhorn to grab both his legs and the pulley at the same time. In one motion, Badeen and Sinkhorn heaved the pulley and Roger, still screaming, into the steaming morass of pulp. Cold silence filled the room.

"They'll find preacher-man when they drain the soup. Too bad he committed suicide," Badeen said to Sinkhorn, "which is what he truly did, because he brung it on himself. He gave me no choice. It's sad, terrible sad." His eyes locked onto Mike. "You got a problem, Ferris?"

Mike could not find his tongue.

"Speak up, man!"

Mike lowered his head. He couldn't look at Badeen. *Poor Roger—good guy—worse than Viet Nam—right here in Freepont. What the hell—*

"Be too bad if you forced me put your wife and kid down."

Mike's head jerked up. Before he could say anything, someone outside thumped on the door. Badeen, followed by Sinkhorn, scrambled down the steps and motioned for Pell to open the door. An angry-looking supervisor in a yellow hardhat charged in.

"Who bolted that door?"

"Cheap thing sticks all the time," Badeen said. "Company ought to replace it." He and Sinkhorn brushed past the supervisor and out the door. Mike glanced at the supervisor. Their eyes met for a fleeting moment before Mike looked away and pushed through the door behind Marvin Pell.

Chapter Seven

Balanced on his bike, one foot on the back stoop, Jason blew "Taps" on his dad's old Army bugle. He knew how to play the mournful tune because his dad had taught him. Just enough breeze kept the mosquitoes grounded and flipped the leaves of the sycamore tree from green side to chalky and back again in a lazy, fluttery rhythm that caught the sunlight with a rippling effect, a perfect Midwestern spring day.

Luke lay in the shade-cooled grass under the sycamore tree twenty feet from the back door. Linda rattled around in the kitchen.

"Supper's overcooked and getting cold. Would you stop playing that bugle? Or at least learn another tune? Sometimes I wish he'd left the dang thing with the Army where it belongs."

"He probably had to work overtime, Mom. Or the pickup broke down again."

"Or an accident."

"Nah. Anyway, Dad won't want much supper. We're going fishing."

"Is that all you ever—here he comes now."

The pickup turned off the road before reaching the driveway. Cutting across the lawn, the tired truck narrowly missed the garden and stopped part way onto the gravel driveway at an angle. Jason swung off his bike to go hitch up the boat trailer. His dad alighted from the pickup, took two steps, wheeled around, and slammed the door. He strode past Jason toward the house at a faster gait than normal with a slight sway in his stride.

"Hi, Dad. The boat's loaded. Everything's ready."

"No fishing tonight."

Jason stayed on his dad's heels up the steps. Something told him not to follow his dad into the house. Instead, he leaned on the metal railing and listened through the screen door. His dad banged his lunch bucket on a counter and dropped into a chair.

"Where's dinner?"

His words seemed a half-beat off. Puzzled, Jason decided to go inside. He pulled the door open and stepped into the kitchen.

After a moment of appraisal, Linda turned to Jason. "Fix a plate and take it outside to the picnic table." When he hesitated, she knitted her brow in her best I-mean-it look.

Jason slowly filled his plate, all the while sneaking looks at his dad. He poured Kool-Aid into a clear plastic glass, stuffed a knife, fork, and paper napkin into his shirt pocket, and nudged the screen door open with an elbow. Luke sidled up to him, panting and salivating. Jason ducked away from the door to the steps and lingered within earshot.

"Where've you been? I was scared to death you had an accident."

"I need a beer."

"I think you've had enough beer, honey."

"I'll drink beer when I feel like drinking beer!"

Jason's head jerked up. His mother stood in the doorway.

"Go to the picnic table like I told you." She closed the inside door.

Jason set his plate on the ground for Luke and got on his bike. He had never seen his dad like this.

When Jason got to the kitchen in the morning for breakfast, he found his mother alone. As usual, the radio blabbered away on the counter.

"Where's Dad?"

"Had to leave early for work."

"What made him so ornery last night?"

"I think he just had a bad day."

"He's never been like that. What's for breakfast?"

"Pancakes."

She sure didn't want to talk, so Jason ate in silence. Only the tag end of the announcer's local news alert caught his ear: *The deceased has been identified as Roger Walker, a foreman with LaFarge Paper. Walker was thirty years old, married, and the father of an eighteen-month-old child. The investigation continues into the death at the plant. We'll bring you further developments as they unfold.*

"Mom, the radio said someone died at LaFarge's."

"I wasn't listening."

"That's what it said. Here comes the bus."

"Better run. Be careful, honey."

"Jeez, I'm just going to school, Mom."

"You can't be too careful."

He rolled his eyes when she hugged him goodbye.

Arriving at Augustine High School, home of the Augustine Saints, Jason approached a knot of his classmates and Sal Cabodi, a chunky junior, in a huddle near the front entrance. Underclassmen could not use the front entrance. Only seniors could enter the school through the hallowed front doors, and God have mercy on any underclassman caught defying the rule.

"My dad says someone killed him," Dave Linz said.

"My uncle says he was a company spy," Larry McGraw said.

Cabodi snorted. "Had it coming if he was a snitch."

"No one has that coming," Jason said.

Cabodi whirled around. "Who asked you?"

Jason ignored the question.

"I asked you a question, Saint Jason the Dick."

"Take it easy, Cabodi," Jason said. "Nobody has the right to kill anyone. Violence never solves anything."

"Ain't you the nicey-nice geek-dork-jerk. Saint Jason, conscientious objector on account of he's a chicken-shit freshman."

Jason swallowed. Heat rushed up his neck and into his face. "Takes a chicken-shit junior to know."

Everybody laughed. Cabodi's jaw dropped.

"What'd you say, you little prick?

"You heard me."

Cabodi shoved Jason against the building just as the first bell rang. Father Ed poked his nose out the door. "You're late, boys. Better move it." Everybody hustled inside, Cabodi elbowing and shoving Jason all the way. With Father Ed directing traffic, even freshmen could enter the front door.

Jason lay in his bed in the dark, wide-awake and thinking about Sal Cabodi. He had never liked Cabodi, but he had never smarted off to him before. Cabodi disgusted him. Why? Because of his stupidity? Because of his greasy, slicked-back hair? Because of the way he bullied people?

All of the above.

He also feared Cabodi; feared his strength and the anger that always seemed to lurk just beneath the surface, as if his skin could barely contain the violence. Besides, Cabodi didn't like him either. They'd probably get into it one of these days. Cabodi would whup him good, but maybe that would put an end to the harassment.

And what about Dad? He sure wasn't the same. Something had changed big-time. Did it have anything to do with the man who died at work? He probably knew the man and felt sad and upset because the man died.

How did he die? Did he fall? Did something fall on him? Did he get caught in a machine?

The man had driven to work in the morning assuming he'd come home that afternoon to his wife and kid, and leave for work again the next morning. Then, just like that, the baby didn't have a father and the wife no longer had a husband. Did the woman have relatives to help her? What would she do for money? No wonder his dad came home so ornery. He probably worried about his own family. What if something like that happened to him?

Jason heard his mother's voice downstairs, but couldn't make out her words. He rolled off the bed and crawled to the landing at the top of the stairs.

"What's eating you, Mike? All you do is stare at the TV

and drink beer. You never drank like this." A long silence followed. "Why don't you take Jason fishing tomorrow after work? I'll fix you a nice lunch to take along."

"If he wants to go fishing, he can go. I don't feel like it."

"At least you could tell me what's going on."

Jason waited for his father to respond. His mother spoke instead. "Well, if you're going to sit there like a zombie, I'm going to make a cup of herbal tea and read awhile. I hope you get over whatever's bugging you. You're not much fun to be around lately."

Jason kept listening. His dad must really be feeling sorry about the man who died, or maybe about the man's wife and kid, to be taking it like this.

Why won't he at least talk about it? Talking might help. Kind of like confession. Not that it would be a confession, but sometimes getting something off your chest and out in the open can help. One of the secondary benefits of confession. Forgiveness is the main thing, but according to Father Ed, the act of verbalizing also provides immediate relief, like shedding a heavy coat on a warm day.

The silence below snaked its way up the stairs to fill the stairwell and the darkness on the landing. Jason quietly returned to his bed, faced the wall, and buried his face in his pillow.

Could he help his dad? No. If he wouldn't talk to his wife, he sure wouldn't talk to his son.

What was Cari doing? He wished she'd play her violin. The night surrounded everything, silent as death, with not even a cricket sawing away or a tree frog croaking. Why were some nights so quiet and others so raucous?

In the morning he heard his mother slamming cupboards and rattling dishes while he dressed. When he entered the kitchen, the newspaper blocked his father from view while his mother fussed at the stove and sink.

"Your dad had eggs, honey. Want some?"

"No, thanks, Mom. Just cereal for me. Want to go fishing tonight, Dad?"

"No."

The silence reminded Jason of a funeral. The kitchen lacked only an organ playing and some awful-smelling flowers. He poured Rice Crispies into a bowl and added two-percent milk.

The headline on the front page of the newspaper on the table asked: *Is plant death a homicide?* He picked up the paper. Beneath the headline, a picture of Roger Walker stared at him.

"Did you know him, Dad?"

"Who?"

"The man who died."

"He worked inside. I'm a yard man."

Why'd he sound so irritated? If he didn't know the man, why act so weird? Jason nodded and ate his cereal. A minute later, his father pushed back from the table, grabbed his lunch bucket, and stalked out.

"Don't bring that up, honey. It upsets him."

"The paper says it was suspicious. And there might've been witnesses."

"It's none of our business."

"I wonder if that's why Dad's been so grouchy."

"Just let it go, Jason. It's none of our business."

Chapter Eight

Tall, a little overweight, and in his mid-thirties, Father Ed Andre had a bald head circled by a fringe of black hair that gave him the look of a monk. In addition to his duties as Director of Religion at Augustine High, he also served as pastor of St. Vincent Church and taught several religion classes at Augustine. He encouraged, even demanded, class participation when he taught. The more his students challenged him, the more he liked it. Up to a point.

Religion was a snap subject that everyone passed. The priests and nuns awarded grades by some mysterious system that Jason often wondered about, although it didn't really matter to him. The subject matter bored most students out of their skulls because they had heard the same stuff since grade school and took it all for granted. Not Jason. He liked religion classes more than any of the others, even better than Sister Alphonsa's English lit class.

The warm spring day beyond the open windows beckoned to everyone inside, except Jason and those who struggled to stay awake, trying with all their might to keep their eyes open. Father Ed always stood at the head of the class and delivered a short lecture before opening the session for discussion.

"So if a priest isn't available for confession, you can make a perfect act of contrition to be absolved. Which means you must be truly sorry that you offended God. It doesn't work to ask for forgiveness to avoid damnation. That would be self-serving and not a perfect act of contrition, but an imperfect act."

Jason raised his hand. Father Ed acknowledged him.

"Father, wouldn't it always be in the back of your mind

that you wanted to save your soul?"

"Not necessarily. Contrition can be pure. When we offend a friend, it isn't difficult to apologize, is it? When we do that, we are in a sense asking for forgiveness for the sake of our friendship. Isn't it natural to express remorse for hurting someone's feelings? Why should it be otherwise when we've offended God?

"A perfect act will always remit venial sins. It will also obtain forgiveness of mortal sins if we resolve to go to confession as soon as possible."

"Sounds like we can't be sure of a perfect act."

"It's important not to get hung up here, Jason. Don't you think God knows what's in your heart? Of course he does. He knows your entire life. Every thought, every act."

"So he hears our prayer in context, not just as an isolated act of contrition?"

"Wouldn't you think so? Of course. More important, your track record would affect the purity of your prayer. We can never fully escape our past actions."

Jason glanced across the aisle. Larry McGraw was sound asleep sitting upright. Two aisles away, Dave Linz's head bobbed and jerked. "Seems to me we could never be certain of forgiveness unless we confessed in the confessional."

Father Ed gazed at Jason. How close was he to cutting off debate? Sometimes it took only a word or a look for him to lower the boom. And why the smile on his face?

Father Ed turned to the white board, picked up a felt eraser and, taking careful aim, bounced the eraser off McGraw's head. Everyone laughed when McGraw woke with a start.

"Good shot, Father!" someone said from the back of the room.

"Good morning, Mr. McGraw," Father Ed said. "So nice of you to join us. Have you had your breakfast yet?"

Embarrassed and still half asleep, McGraw smiled sheepishly.

Father Ed continued as if nothing had interrupted him. "And let us not forget, Mr. Ferris, God's infinite mercy."

31

"That's another thing, Father," Jason said. "How can God's mercy be infinite? Doesn't that destroy the notion of justice? You could do anything and be forgiven."

"A good question. One that theologians have wrestled with for centuries. It's true because God loves us. On the other hand—"

"Doesn't make sense."

"Listen, mister, you can't place human limitations on God."

"Isn't justice another word for fairness? Shouldn't God be fair?"

"Some things will always remain mysteries."

"Seems to me whenever something isn't logical, it becomes a mystery of faith."

The priest bent over and slammed his palm on the desk.

"That's sarcastic and out of line, Ferris! We can discuss these points without that kind of attitude. And what do you think purgatory is about? It's about resolving the attributes of mercy and justice. Now let's move on.

"Mr. McGraw, should we confess venial sins or only mortal ones?"

Caught off guard, McGraw blinked several times. "Just the mortal ones, Father."

"Stake your soul on your answer?"

McGraw, still bleary but getting up to speed fast, swallowed and said, "Well, it's best to confess everything."

"Why?"

McGraw squirmed. "Well, sometimes it's hard to tell which is which, you know? One person's venial could be someone else's mortal. And vice versa."

Father Ed smiled broadly. "Nice bluff, man. You should take up poker. Can anyone inform Mr. McGraw why we should confess even our venial sins?"

No one answered. When it became plain no one would volunteer, Jason raised his hand. Father Ed nodded to him.

"Because confessing our everyday faults helps form our conscience and helps us fight evil inclinations. We need to remind ourselves to keep trying to do better."

"Correct." Father Ed's gaze swept the room. "You all learned that when you studied the catechism for your first communion, just in case you're wondering. Don't forget it." Pausing, he seemed to have another thought. "If you think the catechism is kid stuff, just a bunch of rules that a bunch of monks came up with in a gloomy monastery centuries ago, you are wrong. The catechism is your spiritual road map. It will take you to heaven if you follow the road it lays out."

McGraw raised his hand. "Father, you only hear confessions for ninety minutes a week. Wouldn't it take a lot more time if everyone began confessing every time they teased their sister or talked back to their mom?"

McGraw was a glutton for punishment and knew how to push Father Ed's buttons. A collective twitter filled the room. Father Ed's neck turned red as he glared at McGraw. No one fidgeted or made a sound, like when someone tells an off-color joke with grownups around. Jason laughed inwardly. In the eyes of the class, McGraw, always the rebel, had begun the process of elevating himself to minor sainthood.

"Mr. McGraw, do you have a sister?"

"No, Father."

"Do you sass your mother?"

McGraw twisted in his chair. "Well, yeah, I have once or twice."

Father Ed hovered over McGraw. "Once or twice? Is that all? In fourteen years? Or are you lying?"

Jason noticed the sidelong glances and stifled snickering in the room. Linz did everything short of strangling himself to keep from laughing. McGraw looked totally uncomfortable, maybe even a little scared.

"Yes, Father, I've talked back to my mom more than once or twice."

"So perhaps you should examine your conscience and consider that behavior before entering the box. The fact that you needed to minimize your smart-mouthing of your mother tells me you may have a problem there. Give it some thought, mister."

McGraw peered up at the priest and started to squirm.

Catching himself, he sat stock-still. His Adam's apple jerked when he swallowed.

"One final piece of advice, Mr. McGraw." Father Ed leaned forward and braced himself on McGraw's desk. "You get more sleep at night and let me worry about the confession schedule. Does that meet with your approval?"

"Yes, Father."

"Good."

Relieved laugher accompanied the class bell. Everybody surged to the door. When it opened, Sister Alphonsa's black and white habit filled the door frame. The stampede halted.

"Everybody stand back!" Father Ed commanded as he waded through the crowd to clear a path. "Good morning, Sister." He smiled broadly at the attractive nun, shook her hand warmly, and escorted her, face flushing, into the room.

Nice, Jason thought, that they liked each other.

Chapter Nine

The Cubs and Cardinals battled on TV in a rare Saturday day game while Jason watched and read a book, and his dad watched and drank. Jason looked up and saw a white car turn into their driveway.

"Someone's here, Dad." Jason plopped his book on an end table and crossed over to the front door.

"Who?"

"I don't know. A man and woman. They're dressed up."

Mike, shirtless, remained slouched in his chair. Linda swept into the living room wiping her hands on a dishtowel. She met the visitors at the door.

"Good afternoon, ma'am. I'm Detective Gates." He held his ID and badge out for Linda to see through the screen door. "And this is Detective Pearson."

Linda nodded and opened the door.

"Thank you, ma'am."

While Luke sniffed Gate's pant leg, Jason sat on the bottom step of the stairs.

"We'd like to speak with Mr. Ferris," Gates said.

"Mike, these two want—"

"—to speak with me."

"Mr. Ferris, I'm Detective Gates—"

"—and she's Pearson. How's it going?"

The detectives exchanged glances.

"We need to ask you a few questions," Gates said. "about the incident at the plant."

Mike turned to Jason on the step. "Go outside a while, son."

Jason sprang up and hurried to the kitchen with Luke close behind. "You stay here, Luke," Jason said and slipped

35

out the back door. Once outside, he raced all the way around the house to the front porch, climbed the white railing, and crawled behind a huge rubber plant in a pink wicker basket next to the screen door.

"Mr. Ferris, let me repeat: Someone suggested we see you regarding the death of Roger Walker."

Jason peeked through the screen. His father hadn't moved. The two detectives sat on the sofa. Linda perched on the edge of the other easy chair.

"Why would this person think I was there? Was he?"

"Who said it was a he?" the female detective asked.

"Not many women in that plant."

"Where were you?"

"I'm a yard man."

"We've talked to another man," Pearson said. "A blind man who can see twenty-twenty when he wants to. Isn't that odd?"

Detective Gates interjected. "Who we also think was there when Walker somehow ended up in the pulp tank. We know it wasn't suicide. Suicides don't leave their glasses on the platform next to the tank. They don't have a smashed kneecap either. Why would anyone smash his knee before taking his life?"

"Why're you asking me all these questions? You seem to know a lot."

Detective Gates leaned forward. "You know Badeen?"

Mike reached for his beer. "You guys like a beer?"

"No, thanks."

"Sure I know Badeen. Works at the plant."

"He killed a man fourteen years ago. Thanks to a sharp lawyer and his mother's accident, he got out after eight years," Gates said.

"What's your point?"

"He likes to hurt people, Mr. Ferris. He's beaten two other men real bad. Supposedly in self-defense. Get the picture? And his brother, the guy with one eye, is just as bad or worse. Know how he lost his eye?"

When Mike didn't answer, the detective continued.

"He lost it in a fight he started. Ended up beating the other guy so bad he nearly died. One-eyed Badeen spent time in prison for manslaughter in another case. Does he sound like someone you'd like to tangle with?"

Detective Pearson cut in for her turn. "What about Sinkhorn?"

"What about him?"

"Know him?"

"Sure."

"He's also as bad as Badeen. Probably smarter and just as bad. Far as we know, he never killed anybody before, but he's been in more scrapes than you want to know about. He's a mean one. Any comment?"

Jason pressed his ear to the wall next to the screen door. No one inside said anything until Detective Gates finally broke the silence. "Any idea what kind of trouble you bargain for when you withhold information?"

"Threatened your family?" Pearson said. "That it?"

"I'm telling you, I don't know nothing, damn it. You want me to take a lie detector test?"

"Maybe. Won't change your mind, will you? Sure'd look fishy if you did."

"Okay," Detective Gates said, "let me get to the point. You are a person of interest in this case. Not quite a suspect yet—we're working on that—but you need to know where you stand. That's all I'm saying. You better do some hard thinking, Mr. Ferris."

"Are we done?"

Gates stood up. "For now, yeah."

The female detective arose from the sofa.

"Thank you, Mr. Ferris," Gates said. He nodded at Linda. "Ma'am."

At the door, Pearson turned to Mike. "Can't keep a lid on boiling cabbage, Mr. Ferris. Sooner or later something blows and makes a real stinking mess for everybody. You get scalded if you're too close."

Jason stayed low behind the rubber plant as the two detectives crossed the porch, got into their car, and drove off.

What was going on? No way would his dad hurt anyone. Had he seen how the man died? If it wasn't an accident or suicide, then someone killed him. That's the only reason the police would be involved. Someone murdered that man! A tingly sensation, like when you bump your crazy bone, swept through Jason.

"What's going on, Mike?" Linda said inside. "Did you see what happened? Is that it?"

Jason craned his neck to hear.

"Well, just keep it to yourself then. Just go on being a stranger to your wife and son."

Jason closed his eyes and listened with all his might.

"Tell me, Mike. Please, honey."

Jason had never before heard the next sound that came from the living room. The sound puzzled him at first, until he realized his dad was crying. He peeked through the screen. His mother knelt before his father, holding his hands in hers.

"It's okay, honey. Let it come out."

Crying and gasping, his dad tried to speak. "Two guys, Badeen and Sinkhorn, they threw him into the pulp vat."

"Oh my God!" Her hand flew to her mouth.

"I came in from the yard at the wrong time. They forced me to watch. I just stood there. I shoulda done something."

"And end up in the vat yourself? No!"

"I feel like such a coward."

"Somebody will go to the police."

"Yeah. Me."

"No! They'll come after you. Besides, she said you're a suspect, too."

"For Chrissake, how can I live with this?"

"What about Jason? Is it true what the detective said? Did they say they'd do something to us?"

Mike dragged himself from the chair and paced the room. Jason backed away from the screen door to avoid being seen.

"Promise you won't do anything, Mike. It's in God's hands."

"What's God gonna do? He don't know what goes on in that plant."

"Why'd you bring up a lie detector test? You crazy?"

"That just popped out. I sure as hell didn't say I'd take one."

"Sure sounded like it to me. That Pearson woman thought you did."

"The hell with them and you!"

"They'll be back. Like vultures. Especially Pearson."

"I need a beer."

"Sure, drink yourself to death."

"Might simplify everything."

"Oh, don't get crazy." She said nothing for a few seconds. "Why in God's name did they throw that poor man into the pulp tank in the first place? He must have done something awful."

"Yeah, something awful all right. He kept Badeen from stealing a company ax."

"Just an ax? There must be more to it."

"You don't know those guys."

No wonder his dad had been acting so strange. Witnessing a cold-blooded murder would mess anyone up. If he wouldn't go to the police with what he had seen, the guys who killed the man must have warned him not to. That could mean danger for his wife. Would anyone actually hurt an innocent person, especially a woman? If they'd already committed murder, they'd probably do anything to avoid being caught. So, yeah, they would hurt a woman.

His dad had nowhere to go, no one to turn to. But if his dad and Mr. Pell both talked to the police, wouldn't the police lock up Badeen and Sinkhorn right away until their trial?

Wouldn't a judge or someone keep them there once they heard about the threat to his dad and Mr. Pell? Whoa! What about Badeen's brother? Another badass who'd still be on the loose. Couldn't the police keep an eye on him?

What if he, Jason, approached the police and told them what he had overheard? Maybe that would work. Yet how could he second-guess his dad? That would be disobedience with a capital D. Besides, his dad was smart. If going to the police was the smart thing to do, he'd go.

Jason's jaws tingled. He clenched his teeth and opened his mouth wide to relieve the sensation. He crawled to the porch railing, swung over it to the ground, and decided to take a walk in the woods. The solitude and sounds of nature almost always helped him think and figure things out. Would they work this time?

Chapter Ten

The walk in the woods didn't help. Jason returned home to find his dad still drinking beer and watching television, his mother banging about in the kitchen. Neither of them said a word to him. They didn't know that he had overheard their conversation, but the tension between the two of them filled the house.

Wanting to be alone, Jason decided to read a book; nothing like a good book to provide temporary escape from unpleasant reality.

Once in his room, he didn't feel like reading. He began asking himself the same kinds of questions he had asked earlier. What would his father do? What *could* he do? He had ruled out going to the police. Anybody who would throw a person into a pulp vat had to be more than dangerous; he had to be evil. Such a person would kill again to protect himself.

What if he, Jason, took it upon himself to report to the police? What could he tell them? That he overheard conversations between his mom and dad? Pretty lame. Besides, the police would immediately question his parents, so it would be the same as if his dad had gone to them in the first place. And his dad didn't want to do that, whatever his reasons.

Jason left his room and sat on the rear steps beneath the sycamore tree whose leaves swished and shook in a wispy breeze under a gentle late afternoon sun. Everything looked tranquil and serene in the easy light. How could some people bring so much ugliness into such a beautiful world?

What to do? What if the police caught the killers, tried and acquitted them? Wouldn't they seek revenge? The law had locked Badeen up in prison once for killing a man but had subsequently freed him. Couldn't that happen again, and wouldn't he be even more dangerous the next time? What about Sinkhorn? He had to be as evil as Badeen and just as dangerous the detective had said and maybe smarter.

Jason strode to the garage where the scent of old dry wood mingled with those of oil and gasoline, a combination he always liked. He pulled on the training gloves and began punching the heavy bag while dancing around it as if he were in a ring with an opponent. Left jab, left jab, feint right, another jab followed by a hard right. Back away, move in with the jab, always moving and bobbing.

He continued this for two or three minutes. Then he stood flat-footed and punched the bag with left, right, left, right body shots until sweat soaked his shirt and stung his eyes. His knuckles turned raw and still he punched as hard as he could. Sweat poured from his face to the garage floor. When at last his arms became so weary he could barely raise them, he threw them around the bag and hung on while he gasped for air and his heart raced on. After a while he took a deep breath, unleashed a hard left and right at the bag and backed away, tugging the gloves off his bloody hands.

He returned to his bedroom and fell onto his bed face-down.

His dad was a good man who would want to make things right. Like most normal people, he would follow his natural instinct to do the right thing, the fair thing. Yet, fear for his family and for himself could block that. Wouldn't that make him feel like a coward? His dad had said he felt like a coward. Nobody wants to feel that way. The fear and frustration and anger had to create awful pressure.

Rolling off the bed, Jason reached over to the nightstand for the Ron Santo-autographed baseball his dad had given him. He threw it as hard as he could against the north wall. The ball dented the drywall and dislodged a crucifix, a confirmation gift from his parents, which caromed off the dresser and crashed to the floor.

Falling to his knees, he found the crucifix under his bed. He gasped. The head of Jesus was gone. Not only gone but shattered. What he had thought was metal must have been some sort of composite, maybe partially metal, that had broken apart on impact with the wood floor. With trembling fingers he carefully gathered up the fragments. They were too small to even consider gluing back together. He said a Hail Mary, dropped the pieces into the waste basket, and contemplated the remainder of the crucifix. Throw it away? No, he couldn't do that; it was only partially broken. He reached up and replaced the crucifix on the wall.

He wished Cari would play her violin. More than anything else, he needed to hear the sound of Cari's violin, to know she was there in the dark not far from him. Why wasn't she playing? She played almost every night in her room. Why not tonight?

His dad had already left for work when Jason descended the stairs for breakfast. On the school bus later, Jason gazed out the window and said nothing to anyone.

He attended his morning classes without participating. At noon he drifted off to the football field where he sat under the east goal post and ate the lunch his mother had packed for him.

Countless dandelions poked up into the warm spring air, their yellow blossoms swaying in a playful breeze. Where did the wind come from and where did it go? Why were days hot or not? The meteorologists on TV seemed to know the answers, but did they really?

Dandelions. So beautiful, yet people considered them a nuisance. Why? Who or what determined their weed status to qualify them for eradication? What harm did they do, as opposed to things like poison ivy and poison oak?

People laid down such judgments, but not everybody agreed with them. Dandelions hurt no one. However, what if a person wanted a pristine lawn with no weeds of any kind? What if Mr. Perfectionist lived next door to someone with a lawn full of dandelions because he liked them or thought lawn chemicals were harmful? What if a few dandelions strayed into Mr. Perfectionist's grass to make his lawn look as ugly, in his eyes, as his neighbor's. *Who's right? What's right?*

Murder should be ugly to everyone without exception because it's evil and wrong in every way. How could anyone commit murder and live with himself? Wouldn't a murderer want to turn himself in to the law to pay for his crime and seek redemption? Or were some people just plain evil and unable to think in terms of right or wrong as others did?

Maybe he should talk to Father Ed about what was going on. Father Ed was smart. He'd know what to do.

Deciding he needed to research more deeply the concept of evil before he talked to Father Ed or did anything else, Jason enjoyed the last of his lunch, a chocolate chip cookie his mother had baked. He crumpled the paper bag he carried his lunch in because he never liked to lug a lunch bucket home every day.

He rolled over onto his left elbow and drew a dandelion to his nose without breaking the stem. The delicate slender petals gave off no scent but felt soft and glossy. Why would something so beautiful go to seed after only a few days?

Golden flowers blanketed the open expanse of the football field and beyond. All too soon a sea of gray would replace the gold. Millions of tiny seeds would hold fast as long as they could before falling to the earth to resume the eternal cycle of life and death.

With fifteen minutes remaining until his first afternoon class, he decided to go to the gym to shoot some buckets.

He had just dropped his lunch bag into a trash container outside the equipment room when he heard a scuffle inside.

"Why'd you tell Sister Alphonsa I copied your paper?"

Jason craned his neck to hear.

"You copied it word for word, for crying out loud! Sister spotted it and grilled me. What could I do? She knew I didn't copy yours. I'm not the one repeating freshman English," Dave Linz said, the fear in his voice unmistakable.

Jason barged into the room. Cabodi had Dave up against a locker.

"Hands off, Cabodi!"

Cabodi released Dave, who cowered to the side. Eyes

blazing, fists clenched, Cabodi faced Jason.

"This ain't none of your business!"

"Just let him go."

"Never gonna get laid, priesty? Not even once?"

"You're twice as big as Dave. Think that's fair?"

"What's between him and I is between him and I."

What a dunderhead. Jason's teeth came together. His hands tightened into fists. "How about you and me?" Jason swallowed hard and hoped Cabodi would back off.

A flicker of doubt crossed Cabodi's face. He glanced at Dave, who for some reason was grinning.

"Somebody say something funny? I didn't hear nothing funny."

Dave's smile vanished. Cabodi charged Jason, who sidestepped and tripped him. Cabodi sprawled on the floor but immediately sprang to his feet and crushed Jason against an equipment locker. A punch to Jason's stomach doubled him over. Three shots to his head followed.

Blood streamed from Jason's nose. Cabodi landed another blow to Jason's belly, but when Cabodi tried to hit him with a right to the face, Jason blocked it and hit Cabodi with a hard right to the cheek. Cabodi straightened up for an instant, long enough for Jason to hit him flush on the mouth with a stiff right.

"I give! Don't hit me!"

Jason measured his next blow and blasted his fist into Cabodi's face. Cabodi's nose split. Blood trickled, then poured, from his nostril.

"Stop!" Father Ed said behind Jason, just as Jason drew his right hand back to throw another punch. Father Ed's arm curled around Jason's neck to keep him from hitting Cabodi again.

"Enough!" Father Ed pushed Jason away, grabbed a towel from a shelf, and pressed it to Cabodi's face. "Keep pressure on it, Sal." He turned to Jason. "What the hell's going on here?" He flipped another towel at Jason. "Clean the blood off your face and go to my office. You too, Linz. March!"

As soon as Father Ed got the story from Dave and Jason,

he dismissed Dave and glared at Jason without a word. A large plastic crucifix on the wall behind the priest's desk hovered over them. Would Father Ed sit there all day, or what? Jason stared back until the priest spoke.

"Do you want to know why I'm so disappointed in you? It's because I expect more of you. You've always been so mature. You're a good student and a leader. You might be a bookworm, and the fact everybody knows you want to be a priest sets you apart to some extent. But they look up to you in many ways, inside the classroom and out. You've had a chip on your shoulder lately. And now you close out the school year with a stupid fight. What's going on, Jason?"

"You think it's fair for Cabodi to pick on a little guy like Dave?"

"Look, I know—we both know—that Cabodi is ... Cabodi. I'll deal with him. But you wanted to hurt him. He'd had enough and you wanted to keep hitting him. How many times would you have hit him if I hadn't arrived when I did? Why would you lower yourself to his level? I had no idea you were capable of such violence."

"He's bigger than I am and should be able to take care of himself. He's a no-good jerk. I hate him!"

Father Ed's hand smashed down on the desk. "No! People at times aren't as good as they should be. That doesn't mean they're bad. It doesn't give you the right to hate them or beat them to a pulp! Hate what they do, not them. Where is your Christian humility? Your tolerance. Your charity."

"I guess—"

"Guess nothing! I want your promise this won't happen again. You examine your conscience and make a good confession on Saturday. Do I have your word?"

Jason felt his chest heaving. "Venial or mortal?"

"You decide, mister. Either way, you confess it and mean it. And when you say you're sorry, you'd better be sorry. Don't expect a light penance. Am I clear?"

Jason nodded almost imperceptibly.

"Good. You're dismissed."

Jason wanted to slam the door as hard as he could. He left

it open instead. Maybe bringing Father Ed in on what his dad had witnessed wasn't such a good idea.

He hurried to a lavatory where he scrubbed remaining traces of blood from his hands and forearms. The thought of Cabodi's blood on him made him a little sick. The scrubbing left his knuckles raw. He felt a sliver of guilt for pounding on Cabodi. The guilt didn't rival the pride he felt.

On the way to the bathroom that night, Jason stepped into the hall and saw his dad carrying an armful of clothes and a pillow into the tiny room with a hide-a-bed that served as a spare bedroom when they had company. Jason didn't say anything, but his dad caught his look.

"This heat's been a killer lately, you know? Your mother will sleep better this way."

His dad disappeared into the room and closed the door.

Back in his bedroom, Jason stood at the window. The sound of Cari's violin floated into his room. She practiced a lot because she hoped to get a music scholarship to college. A good thing because her dad drove a truck for the county and probably earned about what Jason's dad did, maybe less. Jason listened until the music stopped.

He knelt, crossed himself, and began to pray. Or tried to. He wasn't quite sure what to pray for or how to start. He knew he wanted more than anything for his dad to be like before. The nuns had taught him the sinfulness of despair. He couldn't help feeling deep down that things would never again be the same with his dad and maybe not with his mother either. He didn't feel sinful, only hopeless.

Cabodi. What a piece of work. Jason had enjoyed punching him. Now the blood and pain he had inflicted haunted his conscience.

The blood. The awful blood.

Rough stuff didn't solve any problems, but maybe the beating would knock some sense into Cabodi. Maybe he'd quit acting like a complete jerk all the time. Why would he pick on a little guy like Dave?

Jason crawled back into bed. Maybe he was sorry he felt

forced to pound on Cabodi, but not sorry that he had done so. Which didn't seem quite right either.

He found it so much more pleasurable to think about Cari. What did she have on? What if she had nothing on, or something skimpy, like maybe panties and something loose and lacy on top?

Did she think of him at night in her room? Did she have the same kinds of thoughts? Did she do what he did when he thought about her? Could a girl do that? How? No way! Then again, maybe that was just one more mystery he didn't understand.

For sure, girls were mysterious; one colossal mystery wrapped around how many little mysteries, God only knew. Just the sight of a girl—any pretty girl, but especially Cari— left a guy wobbly and excited and ready to fight wildcats all at the same time. How could pleasure cause such an exquisite ache? How could such an ache be so pleasurable and yet wrong?

Cari represented the only bright spot. So good-looking and her boobs had really filled out this past year. She looked more like a senior than a sophomore. Thinking about her always aroused him and led to other things that Father Ed admonished him for in the confessional. More than admonished. He got all over his case, like, "Listen up, Jason. Week after week, the same thing. When you say the act of contrition, I want you to mean it. Whatever the occasion is for this sin, you need to avoid it. If it's certain books or magazines, quit reading them. If it's a girl, stop seeing her and stop thinking about her.

"For your penance, ten Our Fathers and ten Hail Marys, one rosary, and attend two weekday masses this week. Now make a good act of contrition."

Father Ed always knew when Jason confessed, even when he tried disguising his voice. Father Ed would address him by name in a voice loud enough to bring the church statues to life. Of course, everyone waiting outside the confessional could hear, too.

A sense of relief always washed over him when they

reached absolution, and he meant it with all his heart and mind when he said the act of contrition: *Oh, my God, I am heartily sorry for having offended Thee, and I detest all my sins because I dread the loss of heaven, and the pains of hell, but most of all because they offend Thee, my God, Who are all good and deserving of all my love. I firmly resolve, with the help of Thy grace to confess my sins, do penance, and amend my life. Amen.*

Then at night thoughts of Cari obliterated all his good intentions.

He didn't like to think about his parents having sex. They did, naturally, but that didn't make it any easier for him to accept. And now his dad slept in a separate room. Not wanting to think about them doing it was one thing. The thought of them not sharing a bed struck him as wrong and unnatural. Married people slept together in one bed. When they didn't, it meant something had gone seriously awry.

Becoming a priest meant taking a lifetime vow of celibacy. Jason recalled the wording of the Code of Canon Law, Canon 277, which he had read many times: *Clerics are obliged to observe perfect and perpetual continence for the sake of the kingdom of heaven and therefore are bound to celibacy which is a special gift of God by which sacred ministers can adhere more easily to Christ with an undivided heart and are able to dedicate themselves more freely to the service of God and humanity.*

Holy Orders supposedly provided the extra grace and power to overcome temptations of the flesh and enable recipients to live chaste lives of service without the distractions of a family. Maybe so, but some priests failed in this respect, a fact that worried him more than anything else about Holy Orders. That's why he read the passage so often. Just like marital vows, ordination vows meant something. They involved honor and pride and commitment. What if he became a priest and failed to live up to his vows?

Chapter Eleven

Jason and Dave had arranged to meet at the Texaco station on West Galen at the edge of town to go bike riding on the first day of summer vacation. Dave lived in town about the same distance from the gas station as Jason did in the opposite direction on Pearl City Road.

They didn't have any particular destination other than stopping for an ice cream cone at the Unified Dairy. They could get anywhere in Freepont in thirty minutes on their bikes.

"Man, isn't summer great?" Dave said as they coasted down Galen Avenue. "No more school, no more homework."

"And then it's always good to get back to school in the fall."

"Are you crazy? Going back's enough to piss off the pope! I wish summer would never end. Remember—" He hit his brakes hard. So hard that his tires squealed and left black marks on the sidewalk.

Jason followed Dave's eyes to three men leaning against a pale blue pickup at the curb just ahead.

"Let's get out of here!" Dave turned his bike around and began pedaling away from the pickup. Jason followed.

"What's the deal?" Jason asked when they had gone a hundred yards or so.

"Man, those guys are bad dudes," Dave said, out-of-breath and red-faced. "The beard's name is Badeen. The bald one is Sinkhorn. The one-eyed guy with all the tattoos is Badeen's brother. My old man and Uncle Jimmie stopped into Mac's Hob Nob last Saturday afternoon. Mac let me stay 'cause I was with the old man. Anyway, these dudes walked in and started drinking beers and shots. My uncle knew who they were and told my dad about them. You wouldn't believe some of the stuff. Man, they are poison!"

Jason recognized the names from when the detectives came to see his dad. He stopped pedaling. "I've never seen poison up close."

"Come on, peckerhead! Let's go!"

Jason turned his bike around, pumped hard to get up to speed, then coasted past the three men, who paid no attention to him. Badeen was huge, well over six feet, with curly blond hair and a short stubbly beard covering a round face.

The man with the shaved head stood much shorter but was even more muscular than the big one.

Badeen's brother was the biggest one. He wore a green tank top and had a black eye patch over his left eye. Tattoos covered his neck and arms.

Jason turned around when he had gone a block past the men. He glanced over at them again as he rolled abreast of the pickup. At that instant, Badeen's blue eyes locked onto Jason's in a way Jason knew he would never forget.

He pedaled hard to catch up with Dave, who hadn't quit riding away from the men. A swirl of images filled Jason's mind, images of his dad and mom and Badeen and Sinkhorn and a man in a pulp vat and a fatherless baby and Father Ed.

"What's with the purse? Is Badeen gay, or what?"

"How should I know?" Dave said and kept pedaling.

At twilight, Jason sat on the back stoop with Luke, whose head was cradled in his lap. One thing about Luke: He loved to have his ears scratched. The only thing he liked better was lying on his back while someone, usually Jason, scratched his ears and slowly rubbed his belly at the same time. He'd fall sound asleep every time.

Jason could not get the sight of Badeen and Sinkhorn out of mind. Knowing what they had done to that man vaulted them from the ordinary to the grotesque. How could anyone do what they did? Most people didn't want to hurt or kill an animal, let alone a human being.

He knew his dad had hunted as a boy and young man but never after Vietnam, according to Jason's mom. His dad never said why, though that wasn't hard to figure out. He said he still liked guns because of their beauty and precision, and he loved to shoot at targets, but no more hunting.

Jason never had a desire to hunt. The thought of killing a rabbit or a deer made him queasy. For some reason that he couldn't quite figure out, he didn't feel that way about fish, though he felt terrible when a fish swallowed a hook. The first time that happened, he pulled the hook out, which was awful because it ripped guts with it and had to be painful to the fish, cold-blooded or not.

After that episode, he always cut the line and left the hook inside the fish if he couldn't dislodge it cleanly. He could retrieve the hook when he cleaned the fish and the poor thing wouldn't have to suffer the pain of having its insides torn out. If he threw the fish back, the hook might become encysted and give the fish a chance to survive.

You couldn't measure the difference between a fish, or even a warm-blooded animal, and a human being. The danger of injury or death always existed in work and sports and even in driving a car. But to plan to destroy a person and then follow through on the plan surpassed all reason and feeling.

He roughed Luke's ears with both hands and hugged him. "Well, Luke, let's go in. I can't scratch your ears all night." Luke raised his head and looked at him, then rolled upright and shook himself when Jason got to his feet. "I've got some reading to do. Let's go, boy."

Indoors, his mother read a magazine while his dad watched TV. An open beer and two crumpled empties lay on the end table next to his dad's chair. Jason paused at the foot of the stairs.

"Good night, Mom. Good night, Dad."

"G'night, son. Sleep tight."

"Want to go fishing this weekend?"

"You know they don't bite in heat like this."

"Larry and Doyle caught a mess of walleye yesterday off the point."

"Jason, what'd I just say?"

Jason looked down at Luke and they both trudged up the

stairs. His mother spoke when he reached the top landing. He knelt and listened.

"That wasn't nice, Mike. You've become a stranger to a kid who adores you."

"Look, like I said earlier, I've got to go, Lin. It's eating my guts out."

"You know everything is black and white with Father Ed. He'd send you to the police."

"I gotta take a chance, Lin. I can't stand it any longer."

"You didn't do anything wrong. What's there to confess?"

"For God's sake, I saw a murder!"

"*You* didn't commit murder! What about Jason? What about me? You said yourself Badeen would come after us. How many times do we have to go over this?" Her hand slapped against her forehead. "Oh! I'm getting a god-awful headache."

Jason, followed by Luke, proceeded into his bedroom and leaned on the window frame with his forehead touching the glass.

The catechism said you had to love your enemies. To hate them was wrong, even sinful. Hate the sin, love the sinner. How could you separate the two? If you liked someone, you liked him because of what he did. His actions defined him and determined what you thought of him and whether you wanted to hang out with him. How could you like what he did and yet not like him? Or vice versa.

Jason fell onto his bed and patted the bedspread. Luke jumped up without hesitation and went limp as soon as Jason began rubbing his belly.

"What would you do, Luke, if I kicked you or swatted you with a newspaper instead of scratching your ears or rubbing your belly? I could say I loved you, but if I treated you mean, you'd stay away and wouldn't like me.

"Why should people be any different? Shouldn't you dislike or hate people if they do bad things? If saying one thing and doing something else equals hypocrisy, doesn't it follow that loving people while hating what they do is a form of hypocrisy? Isn't it natural to hate a person whose actions are hateful? How could anyone expect you to make the distinction between the person and the person's actions? What's your take on this stuff, Luke?"

Luke raised his head at the sound of his name. He gazed at Jason for a moment and poked him with a paw, his signal for Jason to continue with the belly stroking, which Jason resumed doing.

"It's so natural to avoid pain, Luke. Enemies give you pain of one kind or another, so isn't it natural to dislike or even hate them, depending on how much pain? Maybe you have to rise above such a natural reaction? How do you know when to follow your natural inclinations and when to reject them?

"Why should one person's hateful acts cause guilt or a sense of sin in another person for failing to love the one who committed the hateful acts? Having free will means you're responsible for what you do. It shouldn't mean someone else should suffer for what you do."

Jason didn't know the answers and wasn't even sure of the questions. He did know that he couldn't compete with the early fathers and Augustine and Aquinas when it came to theology and morals. He wanted to go to sleep and not think anymore. He curled up with Luke, who fell asleep in no time. Sleep took its time coming to Jason.

Chapter Twelve

The next day at dusk Jason sat on the front porch reading a book, so engrossed that he didn't notice the car on the driveway until the door chunked. He looked up to see a man squeeze his blubbery body out from behind the steering wheel of a green Pontiac. The man glanced over his shoulder before he lumbered up the path to the porch. He wore a LaFarge Paper Company cap. Jason recognized him.

"Your dad home?"

"Yes sir." Jason crossed over to the front door, opened it for the man, and followed him inside. Jason's dad, slumping in his favorite chair as usual, bolted to his feet when he saw the man.

"Hey, Marvin, what're you doing here?"

"We gotta talk, man."

Linda came in from the kitchen.

Jason felt, then saw, his dad's eyes on him.

"Go over to Cari's awhile, son."

Jason had heard about Marvin Pell. Fat, but an outstanding fisherman and boatman who worked at the plant. A year or so ago the paper had run a feature on him for winning a bass tournament.

Jason proceeded through the kitchen and out the back door toward Cari's. Then he retraced his steps to the picnic table on the concrete patio next to the house. Even with the open window, the voices sounded muffled at first. Before long the discussion inside heated up.

"We can't live our life this way!" Mr. Pell said.

"You have to!" Linda said.

"Don't tell me what I gotta do!"

"Pipe down, both of you! Next one yells, gets their ass

55

out of here!"

The voices softened again, but not for long.

"Listen, Mike. There's two of us. With only one witness, it's 'he said-he said.' But not with two. The cops really grilled me. They know Walker didn't jump into the vat by hisself, and they think I had something to do with it. You can bet that supervisor who barged in told the cops what he thinks.

"I tell you, the police know Badeen and Sinkhorn did it, and they suspect you and me, too. We'd better tell them our story before we get in so deep we can't get out."

Mike drained the last swallow of beer and crushed the can.

"So let's think about this, Marvin. We go to the cops. Maybe they believe us, maybe they don't. Let's say they do. They round up Badeen and Sinkhorn, who deny it or tell the cops you and me killed Walker. Maybe to be on the safe side the law rounds up all of us and keeps us locked up. What's your family going to live on? What about mine? Or maybe they hold those guys and let us go. What about Badeen's brother? They can't haul his ass to jail. How you going to protect your family? You think the law can do it? Give me a break!"

Nobody said anything for a few seconds as Jason strained to hear. There wasn't a sound until Mr. Pell said in an even voice, "Maybe we need to take them out ourself."

"Sure. Just like that we take them out. Maybe, for the sake of argument, we get the job done. Then the law dumps us in the slammer, and we might as well be dead for all the good we can do our families."

"What if the law never finds out?"

"For the love of Christ, Pell, you're making me tired! You had much experience killing people? About as much as I've had. All we can do is keep our mouth shut."

"You want to live like this? I don't!"

"If you're not men enough to do something," Linda screamed, "then live with it! Oh, this damn headache is splitting my skull!"

"It ain't that easy, woman!"

56

"Complaining to me won't help, fat stuff!"

"Kiss my ass!"

"That's it, Marvin! Out!"

The fat man charged out the door. He waddled to his car, wedged himself in, and sped down the road.

Jason rolled onto his back on the picnic table and, arms outstretched, stared at the darkening sky. Nothing made sense. You read about this kind of stuff in the newspaper or saw it in movies, not right here in Freepont where normal people lived.

What could his dad do next, if anything? He clearly needed to tell somebody, had to unburden himself. How could he do that without taking a big risk? His own wife was dead-set against him telling anyone, even a priest, and man, was she becoming a nag, or what? Not that anyone could blame her. She wasn't healthy in the first place and not exactly a pillar of strength when things bumped along okay and normal, not to mention this kind of weirdo stuff.

Darkness seeped into the spaces separating buildings and trees and everything else as Jason lay on the table lost in thought and non-thought, mostly the latter. Questions without answers pricked him like darts from every direction, while images of Cari kept intruding. He welcomed those, and before many minutes had passed, thoughts of Cari fought off the questions and concerns relating to his dad and what had happened at work.

By turn, she swirled into his imagination fully dressed, barely clothed, or naked. When he saw her dressed, he dwelled on slowly removing every piece of her clothing, wondering and imagining all the while what she would say and what he would say. Or maybe they would say nothing. He had often touched her arms and hands as they horsed around. What would her breasts feel like? What would she feel like down there beneath her flat belly?

Once, when she pretended to do the limbo under the old swing in her backyard, he had seen the mound below her pelvis where her thighs converged. The bulge against her shorts instantly aroused him, and he turned away so she wouldn't notice. She asked him what was wrong, so he made a dumb joke to deflect her, but something in her voice told him she knew why he had turned. She was so smart and beautiful and observant.

He didn't even have to touch her. When her bare arm got next to his, he always felt something like static electricity and could feel his skin and body hair reaching out for her. Did she feel that too?

He knew that fantasizing about Cari was wrong, that he would have to confess his impure thoughts and all the rest to Father Ed, who would admonish him and give him ever more elaborate penances: Our Fathers and Hail Marys, entire rosaries, extra masses, chores around the church and rectory. Then they would recite the Act of Contrition together and he would vow not to repeat his sins.

He knew he would, though, which caused him to worry about the validity of his confession, knowing he would be unable within a day or two to resist the ache of longing that would permeate his body and imagination until he couldn't stand it.

A car horn honked twice. Jason leaned up on his elbows on the picnic table. The horn blared three more short bursts.

His mother's voice broke the silence inside the house. "For crying out loud, who's making that racket?" The sound of her footsteps tapped through the open window as she hurried to the front door. "It's a pickup. In our driveway."

"It's someone from work," his dad said a moment later. "Stay here."

The screen door to the porch opened. Jason rolled off the table and said, "Stay, Luke. Stay!" He dashed around the corner of the house, angled wide through Cari's dark lawn and along the far side of the garage. A pale blue pickup, its headlights off, had stopped at the edge of the faint pool of light from the yard lamp at the peak of the garage. Breathing hard, Jason stayed in the shadows behind the north corner of the garage as his dad approached the pickup.

"Heard you had a meeting here," a man said inside the truck.

"Marvin stopped by, that's all."

"Don't give me no baloney, Ferris."

Mike scuffed the gravel with his shoe. Luke sidled up to him. He bent over to pat the dog.

"No more meetings."

"You don't have to worry about me."

"How's that boy of yours?"

"You leave my family out of this."

A man swung out of the pickup.

Badeen!

Jason's heart pounded. He tried to swallow. His mouth had gone dry, his legs wobbly.

Badeen grabbed Mike. He slammed him against the truck and slapped him across the face. Luke growled. Badeen kicked the dog hard. Luke yelped and slouched off into the darkness, yipping and whining.

"I was a guest in the big house once. Ain't goin' back. Your family don't mean nothing to me."

Jason, his temples throbbing, stepped out of the shadows behind his dad and edged into the periphery of light. Badeen's eyes locked onto him.

"I got a son, too," Badeen said, his eyes still on Jason. "He lives with his ma. She's a witch. He's a good kid."

He kept looking over Mike's shoulder at Jason. When Mike tried to twist around to see what Badeen saw, Badeen restrained him.

"Look at me, Ferris, and listen real close. I'm not a bad person. Walker forced me to do what I did. I felt real bad about it. Still do. But I do what I need to, just like you. So don't get stupid. I honest-to-God hate to hurt people. It makes me sick."

His glare darted to Jason, who stood his ground and stared back. After a long moment, Jason retreated into the shadows without a sound. He knew, regardless of what Father Ed or the catechism said, he would never forgive Badeen for slapping his father or for kicking Luke.

"So don't mess with me and we'll get along good. Understand?"

Mike stared at Badeen in silence. Badeen released him, climbed into his pickup, and started the engine. He dumped the clutch in reverse and peeled gravel all the way to the hard road, then tore off to the east.

Mike didn't move. He stood staring up into the deep dark sky as if looking for answers to questions he couldn't begin to form or comprehend. He headed for the house.

Jason swallowed a lump in his throat and wished his dad would move them all far, far away to a place where Badeen could never find them, where they could start all over. He hated Badeen and Sinkhorn. He wished they would die terrible deaths, especially Badeen.

Jason walked across the lawn to the county road and turned left. Clouds intermittently obscured a brilliant full moon. The cool night air filling his lungs carried a scent of lilac, a *taste* of lilac. A few yards farther west, the frisky breeze carried the sweetness of honeysuckle, which Clem Ferguson's bees thrived on.

Night created a different world in so many ways. The lack of visibility provided clarity. The quiet darkness fostered thinking.

How many times had Father Ed insisted that Christians had to love their enemies? Too often to count. Why? Because Christ had. Even those who killed him: *Father, forgive them, for they know not what they do.* His love was unconditional and infinite; he commanded his followers to emulate his example; therefore, logic dictated that they love, certainly not hate, even those who hurt them.

The more subtle scent of clover replaced the sweetness of honeysuckle. The breeze quickened ever so slightly.

Was God's love unconditional? Father Ed and the catechism maintained that unrepentant sinners would, or at least could, go to hell forever. So God's love *did* have a limit; it *was* conditional. If a person didn't repent and *ask* for forgiveness, he was lost. Forgiveness had to be requested and granted, or the sinner had no hope. Which seemed reasonable enough.

Would he—could he—forgive Badeen and Sinkhorn for killing Mr. Walker? Forgive Badeen for slapping his dad? No. Never. But so what? Would Badeen ever tell Jason he was sorry and ask his forgiveness? Not a chance. Why then must Jason forgive him? If God forgives only after someone humbly asks for forgiveness, by what stretch of logic or faith could he, Jason, be bound or even expected to be more compassionate, more forgiving than God?

Should a brother's compassion exceed a loving father's? How could any mortal's compassion exceed God's, or even approach it, if God's love and mercy are infinite?

Jason stopped in the middle of the asphalt road. With clouds blocking the moon, not a glimmer of light penetrated the darkness. A snarl nearby, accompanied by a squeal of pain and thrashing in the undergrowth, sent a shiver through him. He scurried down the asphalt road in the blackness toward home.

Chapter Thirteen

The weeks dragged on. On the last day of June, as Jason watched from the front porch, Father Ed turned his blue Chevy into the driveway. Luke loped down the porch steps and sniffed the priest's trouser legs thoroughly before losing interest because no doggie treats were forthcoming.

"Well, Jason, have you thought about our last discussion?"

Jason had asked the priest a week ago why God had created evil.

"He didn't," Father Ed had said. "Human beings did by using their free will." He had suggested that Jason read what St. Augustine had written about evil.

Luke climbed the porch steps and plopped down next to Jason.

"St. Augustine says evil doesn't exist," Jason said.

"Are you sure he says that?"

"Well, he says evil has no substance, just the absence of good."

"Now you're getting at it."

"He said evil is real. If it's real, doesn't it have to exist, Father?"

"Part of this is semantic. Evil is real to the extent a person chooses something other than good. The potential for evil enables us to be virtuous. How could we recognize heroism without the possibility of cowardice? Or faithfulness without the possibility of infidelity? Wouldn't we be mere automatons? If we didn't possess the moral freedom to choose right or wrong, how could we even strive to become more Christ-like?

"God gifted us the power to ennoble or degrade

ourselves. He threw the ball squarely into our court. Fascinating, don't you think, that God created us free in a far more profound sense than our own Declaration of Independence and Constitution use the term? Pretty awesome stuff."

"To choose evil means it's there. I can't choose something that's not there."

Father Ed tilted his head back and ran his tongue over his lips as he gathered his thoughts. He reached down to scratch Luke's ears again. Luke responded by rolling over, an invitation for a belly rub. When the belly rub didn't materialize, Luke raised his head and peered at the priest.

"Let me try to articulate this. When we opt for a lesser good, or opt not to do good at all, but rather something bad, it's a privation of good, just as darkness is a privation of light. I believe God allows evil in our world, at least for a time, so that by struggling against it we might become better and more in his image.

"And you know what, Jason? Good old Luke here has no more idea what we're talking about than that oak in your front yard. Would you concede, with all due humility, that God in his omniscience is so far superior to us that we will never in this world begin to comprehend these matters? Aren't we to God, intellectually, what Luke is to us?"

"Can't argue with that, Father. Sometimes, though, I think Luke is smarter than some people. I know he's better than a lot of people."

Father Ed laughed. "You might be right. Someone once said that if heaven has no dogs, he didn't want to go there. Tough to argue with that."

The priest withdrew his car keys from his pocket as if to leave, then appeared to have another thought. "Analogies can take us only so far," he said, "but try to think of sin and evil in terms of a fun-house mirror. Have you ever seen yourself in one of those curved mirrors?"

"Sure. They have them at the county fair every year."

"The image you see is distorted reality. The image is there, but it's only a reflection that has no existence of its own.

Likewise, evil has no existence without good. So let's talk in concrete examples. Sex is good, a gift from God that people can distort or corrupt. People can abuse alcohol or, for that matter, food. Doesn't mean those things are intrinsically bad."

"So circumstances can make a difference?"

"Circumstance and motive can enhance or despoil our actions, yes."

Jason nodded and then frowned. "That's like saying the end justifies the means."

"No, no. A good end never justifies immoral means. You can rationalize that idea all day long; it never bears up under scrutiny." He fiddled with his keys for a moment. "To get back to the separate existence of evil, let's use the ultimate example: the taking of life. As odious as I find capital punishment, I must concede that a legitimate government has the rightful power to levy the death penalty for certain heinous crimes, assuming of course, that due process is followed to the nth degree.

"Killing in self-defense and in a just war, as despicable as both are, is allowable. Otherwise it's one of the worst of mortal sins. Not only does it deprive a person of his life on earth, it could well cost him his salvation."

"I don't understand."

"The victim could be in a state of mortal sin. Sudden death wouldn't allow him time to repent. Serious stuff, Jason. Well, I have to run. Please say hello to your folks for me. Are you serving this Sunday?"

"Nope. Next week."

"See you then."

"Okay, Father. So long."

Jason found it impossible to resume reading after Father Ed left. He wanted to think about what the priest had said until it made sense. No doubt it did, but some things you had to really think through.

Lost in thought, he gazed across the road at nothing in particular. Mr. Ferguson tended his bees in the field adjacent to the road. The old man moved deliberately so as not to agitate the bees as he inspected the hives. Before long the bees would start gathering nectar at a furious pace to fill the combs with honey by autumn, a cycle of activity that according to Mr. Ferguson began before man appeared on earth.

Jason picked up the book he'd been reading, Willa Cather's novel *Death Comes to the Archbishop,* about bygone days in the Southwest. He liked the story and Cather's writing style, although some of the characters, especially a few of the priests, disgusted him.

Cather sounded so authentic that it was hard to believe she wasn't Catholic. Raised a Baptist, she had become an Episcopalian who seemed to have great reverence for the Catholic Church.

After a few minutes of reading, Jason closed the book and stared into the distance once more. The fun-house mirror illustration intrigued him. It lacked something, but darned if he could quite put his finger on the missing element.

Freepont's Fourth of July featured a parade down Walnut to Main and ended near the old railroad depot that hadn't seen passenger traffic for decades. Jason liked the parade, but the real fun happened about nine o'clock at night when the fireworks began.

Cari's folks had decided to skip the fireworks this year. Cari would join Jason and his parents to watch the display at the country club on Park Boulevard.

"We'll pretend we're country clubbers," Mike joked when they piled into the old Plymouth. Jason smiled at his dad's first hint of good humor since the trouble began.

The fireworks didn't impress Jason as much as they had in the past. Two distractions got in the way. He couldn't quite shake Badeen from the edges of his mind. That was the bad distraction. The good one sat next to him on a blanket a little behind and to the side of his parents. She brushed against him regularly with an elbow or shoulder or leg. Once, her breast grazed his arm. The touch took his breath away. From then on his sky-high anticipation had nothing to do with the next burst of color in the sky and everything to do with hoping she would do it again.

Or had it been accidental? Probably, he decided, but by this time his imagination dwarfed anything that could light up the night.

Finally, the grand finale thundered and blazed above them, the best he had ever witnessed, starburst upon starburst, along with the explosion of firecrackers that sounded even bigger than cherry bombs and M-80s. At the conclusion, they gathered up their blankets to leave.

"Wow!" Jason said. "That was great!"

"Too many loud ones," Cari said. "I don't like the ones that sound like bombs."

"They're the best! Bet old Luke's under the porch."

When they piled into the car, Mike playfully bumped Linda. "Let's go to the Unified Dairy for some ice cream. Doesn't that sound good?"

Linda nodded and smiled her agreement.

"All right!" Jason said, his chest swelling to see his dad's good mood continuing.

The snarled traffic bottled them up for nearly thirty minutes. After that it took them only ten minutes to drive across town to the dairy. Judging from the crowd, many others thought it was a good night for ice cream.

"What does everyone want?" Jason's dad asked. "Mom and me both want chocolate, for sure. What about you guys?"

"Vanilla for me," Jason said.

Cari rolled her eyes. "Haven't you heard, Jason? They've invented other flavors over the last hundred years. You might try one someday."

"Only monkeys and weird sophomores order banana every time."

"For your information, I'm now a junior."

"Tell him to swing from a tree," Linda said to Cari with a laugh. "Banana for you?"

"Yes, thank you."

"Your great-grandparents must've lived in the Congo."

Cari punched him on the shoulder. "The Dairy has the best banana ice cream in the world. They make their own, you know."

"Whoop-dee-do!"

On the way home after ice cream, Cari leaned against Jason in the back seat, her forearm on the seat against the side of his knee. He had earlier detected the fragrance of her cologne or perfume. Now the scent wrapped around him like something straight from paradise.

"You okay? You're awfully quiet," Cari whispered.

How could he speak when he couldn't trust his voice? Her forearm touching his leg caused his throat to tighten and made his breathing shallow. He feared his voice would squeak. The memory of the night on the swing when she wanted him to kiss her left little room for other thoughts. That, and her shoulder against his and her arm touching his knee. Brushing against him might have been accidental. Not this. No way.

Should he hold her hand? No, you can't want to be a priest and go around holding a girl's hand. Yet....

He had just touched her hand when the headlights illumined the Ferris mailbox. The car turned into the driveway. His dad hit the brakes hard.

"What's that?" his mom asked.

His dad switched off the headlights and shifted into park. "Wait here!" He leaped from the car and ran toward the garage. Sliding from the back seat, Jason followed step for step.

"Go back to the car!" his dad said too late. There on the driveway in front of the garage lay the front half of Luke: head, front legs, chest. Ribs poked out through torn flesh. Entrails spilled onto the gravel. Luke's tongue lay limply on the ground from the side of his mouth, his teeth bared in final agony.

"Oh, God," Jason's dad gasped.

Jason pursed his lips and grimaced, trying not to cry. He heard his mother and Cari approaching. Both of them screamed. Linda embraced Cari.

"Take the kids inside, honey," his dad said.

"What are you going to do?"

"Look for the rest of him."

"I'm going to help," Jason said.

"Jason, listen—"

"I'm going to look."

His dad nodded. "I'll take your mother in and check out the house. You get the flashlight from the car. I'll bring the one from the house."

While Linda and Cari followed his dad inside, Jason retrieved the flashlight from the car's glove box. They searched the property without success.

"Son, you go east along the hard road. Check the ditches on both sides. I'll go the other way."

As if in a trance, except for his thumping heart and erratic breathing, Jason followed the road for a half-mile to a crossroad before he reversed course on the opposite side of the road. His dad waited with two shovels. Whoever had killed Luke had not wanted the rest of him found.

"Where do you want to bury him, son?"

Jason thought for only a second before answering. "Under the sycamore by the back door. I have to go to my room first."

He disappeared inside and returned with a blue flannel shirt. After removing Luke's collar, he wrapped the shirt around him and carried him to the backyard near the sycamore tree.

By the light from the kitchen window, they dug a hole thirty inches deep. Jason stroked the dog's head and smoothed his ears. Barely any warmth remained in Luke's half-body.

Cari joined them.

"I want to say goodbye to Luke," she said. When she knelt down and petted Luke, she began to cry. "Poor Luke. I'm so sorry, Luke. Who would do such a thing? You were the best dog ever. We'll miss you always."

Sobbing, she leaned on Jason's shoulder as she got to her feet, hugged him, and ran home.

"I want to bury Luke alone, Dad."

"Okay, son." He laid his hand on Jason's shoulder. "I'm so sorry about this. I…." He shook his head and left Jason alone with Luke.

Jason gently laid Luke on the floor of the hole and began to backfill the grave. He carefully rolled the dirt off the first dozen scoops until the dirt covered Luke. After that, he threw the dirt in methodically, tamping it with his feet until he had replaced all of it. He used the hose next to the stoop to clean both shovels before returning them to the garage.

He proceeded upstairs without speaking to his parents. After showering, he shuffled to his bedroom where he prayed at bedside for Luke and for his parents. Cari played her violin across the way, a song Jason had not heard before.

He stood at his window for a long time listening to the wistful music wavering through the unknowing night, knowing Cari was as distraught over Luke as he was. He felt it through the music and knew she did, too.

When the music ended and he climbed into bed, he couldn't sleep. Luke had suffered unspeakable pain, pain that no animal should ever experience. Who had done it and how? With what kind of instrument?

He felt certain of the *who* part, if not the rest. He hoped it had been quick, suspected it hadn't, knew it could not have been quick enough.

Luke, always on the lookout for a treat or to get his ears scratched, would have shimmied up to anyone who hadn't treated him meanly. Badeen had kicked him that night when he slapped Jason's dad, so Luke would have stayed away from him. And one person could not hold a dog and cut him in half. There had to be at least two people.

Luke had never seen Sinkhorn. Maybe Sinkhorn had enticed him and then the two of them had done it. They would have strapped a leash on him, and maybe a muzzle, and then somehow tied him down. Otherwise, Luke would have panicked and become a twisting fury of paws and teeth. And then what? A cleaver or machete? Chain saw? They needed something to cut through the ribs and spine.

No matter the details, someone had butchered Luke alive—slowly, in all likelihood, given the nature of the suspects. If they had just wanted to kill Luke, they could have clubbed him or shot him. A gunshot on the Fourth of July would not have aroused undue curiosity or alarm. No, whoever tortured and killed Luke wanted to send a message.

And by leaving only part of Luke behind they had compounded the cruelty.

Jason rolled off the bed, his T-shirt and boxer shorts damp with sweat. He groped his way down the stairs and through the house to the kitchen where he quietly opened the back door and slipped out to the landing. He felt his way to Luke's grave and sat on the grass next to it. Prayer wouldn't come when he tried to pray.

"Oh, Luke. I'm so sorry I didn't protect you. You really were the best dog ever."

He had vowed not to cry and nearly succeeded as he lay face down across the fresh grave. He didn't make a sound while tears ran down his cheeks. Staying prone for a long time, not caring if he saw another day, he silently grieved for poor Luke.

When the tears stopped, he rubbed his eyes and returned to his bed. He still couldn't sleep right away. Just as he began to drift off, he heard the same sound from the spare bedroom that he had heard that day after the detectives had left, the sound of his father crying. Then: "God, I can't take it any more! If you're up there, tell me what to do!"

His father broke down again, his sobbing calling to mind some poor creature in intolerable pain. No violin, no light, no warmth of embracing arms could dispel the pain and cold despair in that small bedroom where his father lay, alone and scared and without hope.

Chapter Fourteen

In the first seconds of waking, Jason prayed that last night had been a black dream that would recede and disappear forever. Poor innocent Luke should not have been left alone outside. They should have locked him in the house.

Judas despaired and took his own life after betraying Christ. Did he feel like this?

Jason didn't want to leave his bed, didn't want to face the day, did not want to see Luke's grave again. He swore he would shed no more tears, in spite of last night's horror. He would tough it out.

Fantasies about Cari and sleep had provided escapes in the dark of night and had postponed the inevitability of morning. No escape existed in full daylight.

He forced himself to throw the covers back, get dressed, and go downstairs. As if they dwelled in their own separate worlds, nobody said anything of consequence while preparing for ten-thirty mass. Their usual Sunday noon meal, a pot roast, simmered in the crock-pot.

They usually sat midway in the church. Today, they arrived late, so they had to take a pew near the front. Jason knew his dad felt uncomfortable so far forward.

Mass proceeded as usual. They all knelt and stood and voiced the appropriate responses. Jason knew his mom and dad felt just as numb as he did.

Father Ed finished the consecration and distributed the bread and wine to the lay ministers. Jason envied the altar boy and altar girl sitting on a bench near the door to the sacristy. He would serve next week, the highlight of his week, something he would do every week if given the choice.

People rose from their pews and streamed down the aisle

to receive communion. Because of their location in the front of the church, the Ferris family received before most others. Returning to his pew, Jason's dad clutched his throat.

"Dad! What's wrong?"

Mike bent over and tried to suck in air. Jason realized the problem. He pounded his dad on the back. Nothing happened. His dad made an awful gagging sound. Jason wrapped his arms around his chest. He pulled his dad towards him and squeezed with all his strength. His dad gasped. The host flew from his mouth and landed in a wet heap on a pew.

His chest heaving, Mike wiped his mouth and eyes.

Father Ed reached his side. "Are you all right, Mike?"

"Yeah, thanks, Father. I'm okay."

Father Ed motioned to the servers. "Please get Mr. Ferris a glass of water. And bring me a clean finger towel and some holy water." Turning to Mike, he said, "Would you like to receive again?"

Embarrassment showed on Mike's face.

"No, thanks, Father."

Father Ed took the finger towel from the altar girl, wrapped the towel around the wafer, and wiped away all remnants of it from the pew. He finished by sprinkling a few drops of holy water where the host had landed, making the sign of the cross, and blotting the holy water with the towel. He patted Mike on the shoulder before returning to the altar.

Back home, Mike changed into jeans and a red T-shirt.

"I'm going to take a walk before we eat," he said and disappeared out the back door. Jason watched him hunching over Luke's grave. After several minutes, he tilted his head back to look up into the blue sky of a perfect summer day. Then he marched off toward the hard road with extended, purposeful strides.

"We'll eat in twenty minutes," Linda called to him. He waved in reply.

"Is Dad okay?" Jason said. "He's acting totally weird."

Without replying, his mother threw a dishtowel over her shoulder, reached for a bottle of aspirin, and chewed three of them down. She looked as worried as Jason felt.

When his dad returned from his walk, he gathered them all at the kitchen table and prayed over the meal. Normally Jason could never get enough of the pot roast his mother cooked nearly every Sunday. Not today. The food not only didn't smell good, it caused his stomach to roil. He asked to be excused from the table.

His first impulse was to go outside, but he decided to spend the day in his room reading *The Sun Also Rises*, a book he had begun two days ago. He liked the book, although he didn't fully understand it and would have to read it again someday. He lingered in the kitchen.

His dad, apparently not hungry either, had eaten about half his meal when he pushed back from the table and got to his feet.

"Even a deaf man can hear God when He yells. I gotta go."

"Where, Dad? Can I come?"

"No!"

The hurt must have shown in Jason's face. His dad hugged him.

"I need to go alone, son. Didn't mean to bark at you."

"It's okay."

"It ain't okay. Nothing is okay. You stay here and take care of your mother, hear?"

"Sure, Dad."

"I'm right here, in case you forgot," Linda said. "Where *are* you going?"

Mike continued holding Jason. When he released him, he embraced Linda and held her in a way Jason had never seen before. Without a word, Mike left the house and climbed into his pickup. Jason ran out to the yard as the pickup headed down the road and droned from sight.

He decided to see Cari before going to his room to read. He could read later. Right now he wanted to see Cari. More than anything else in the world, he wanted to see Cari.

Two young boys poked through the brush along a creek.

One carried a fishing rod and a tackle box, the other a rod and a stringer of fish. The one with the fish looked up. His eyes widened. He dropped the fish.

"Look!"

"Holy crap!"

Ahead of them in the distance, at the end of rope, a body in a red shirt hung from a railroad trestle.

Cari held Jason's hand while they sat on her porch swing, her eyes moist with tears.

"We'll always have our memories of Luke," she said. "Such a wonderful dog."

Feeling his own eyes welling up, Jason said nothing.

"He was so lovable. God, Jason, it would take a monster to do something like that."

He nodded. Noticing Cari's tears, he decided to change the subject. He couldn't bear seeing her so sad. "I've heard you like Don Parker."

"You're just saying that to change the subject and tease me."

"No, I'm not."

She punched him on the shoulder. "You are, too."

"No, no kidding."

"Who said? They're dirty liars!"

"I don't know, just heard it."

"Well, he is cute, but he's so stuck on himself. Where's your mom going in such a hurry?"

Linda sprinted to the garage with her apron still on. A moment later, the green Plymouth hurtled from the garage in reverse. Swerving, the car slammed against the side of their fishing boat and roared off.

"Aw man, she killed our boat. We'll have to get a new one. Dad'll be totally ticked off."

"Gosh, I've never seen your mom drive like that before."

His mother wouldn't allow Jason to see his father's body before the undertaker had done his work. Meanwhile, the house became a hive of activity. Neighbors and friends swarmed in to see Linda and offer their help. Jason had never seen so much food.

He didn't want to see or talk with anybody, not even Cari. After his mother and Father Ed told him what happened, he spent the rest of the day and most of the next riding his bicycle aimlessly on country roads and through residential areas of town. When people he knew saw him and called out, he ignored them and peddled away as fast as he could.

The July heat and humidity clung to him like a shroud. He drank deeply and often from the water bottle affixed to the frame of his bike. He didn't eat for two days. How could he possibly eat? His father had choked on the communion host and had taken his life after eating his favorite Sunday meal. The thought of food disgusted Jason. So did the thought of crying. Anger and devastation ruled out crying. He would not cry. Wouldn't, wouldn't, wouldn't.

The best guy ever, his dad. A fun guy. No one enjoyed joking and teasing more than he did, at least before the deal at the plant happened. He hadn't gone fishing or taken Jason target shooting since Badeen and Sinkhorn had killed poor Mr. Walker. And he never kidded around after that either, except on the night of the fireworks.

In the past, his dad had taken them for Sunday drives on the west end of town to look at the homes of people with money. They would pick their favorites and imagine themselves living in such grand places. Jason always joined in, offering and defending his own opinions. His all-time favorite, a huge white mansion with pillars, stood on what must have been a two-acre lot.

Every time he said he wanted to live in that house, his father said, "You'll have to mow the lawn, just like now," and Jason countered, "We'd have so much money we'd have it mowed," and his dad would say, "Yeah, well, you'll have to pay for it out of your pocket, not mine," and they'd all laugh.

Now the houses looked gloomy and foreboding. He wouldn't live in one if somebody gave it to him.

Whether walking or biking, he used to daydream and think and sightsee. The solitude had appealed to him then.

Now his mind raced in a loop. Thoughts and fantasies jumbled in his head, had no continuity, popped in and out like fireflies winking in the dark.

Places and people and vehicles flew past him in a blur without registering. The solitude that had appealed to him in the past had changed to emptiness.

One thought and one feeling did register. He knew without doubt that his life would never be the same again, and he sensed he would never again be as happy as before this summer.

On the third day, it dawned on him that beyond his own sense of loss there was something equally serious to worry about: his father's soul. He grabbed his catechism and read: *Suicide is seriously contrary to justice, hope, and charity. It is forbidden by the fifth commandment.*

Lying face down on the grass in his backyard, Jason closed the catechism and rolled over onto his back. Low-hanging, raggedy gray clouds churned in slow motion against small patches of blue sky that could not quite overcome the overcast. He glanced at his watch. Father Ed would arrive in thirty minutes.

Two robins fussed nearby. When their shrieking intensified, Jason leaned on an elbow to see what caused the ruckus. A male and female flitted from limb to limb, screeching their hearts out.

Then Jason heard the bleat of a young robin. Listening intently, he heard it again. By the third time, he spotted the bird clinging to a low branch of a holly bush next to the sycamore tree near the back stoop. The bird appeared ready to fly, though perhaps not well until its wings strengthened.

The adult robins' cries exceeded the crisis of the baby's flying predicament. Surveying the area, Jason saw the real cause of the commotion: an orange cat about thirty yards away, hunkered down low against the ground as it approached. The cat hadn't seen the baby bird yet, or it would be running for the kill. The cat stopped, tensed, and broke into a run toward the bush.

Jason scrambled to his feet and sprinted to the bush. He

and the cat arrived at the same time. The cat, so intent on its prey that it didn't see Jason, leaped at the bush. Jason dove headfirst. Sliding on his belly, arms outstretched, he bumped the cat on the flank just enough to throw it off target. With a vicious snarl, the startled cat raced away and disappeared.

Out of breath and a little shaky, Jason brushed off his clothes. The terrified baby robin still clung to its perch. The adults had retreated to the sycamore tree where they continued their frantic chirping. Jason returned to his catechism and resumed reading: *Suicide contradicts the natural inclination of the human being to preserve and perpetuate life. It is gravely contrary to the just love of self. It likewise offends love of neighbor because it unjustly breaks the ties of solidarity with family, nation, and other lawful societies to which we continue to have obligations. Suicide is contrary to love for the living God.*

And yet: *Grave psychological disturbances, anguish, or grave fear of hardship, suffering, or torture can diminish the responsibility of the one committing suicide.*

Further: *We should not despair of the eternal salvation of persons who have taken their own lives. By ways known to Him alone, God can provide the opportunity for salutary repentance. The Church prays for persons who have taken their own lives.*

The last passage relieved Jason's misgivings about the state of his father's soul, but another question materialized: What about the person or persons who caused the anguish that led to a man committing suicide? How did God deal with them? Shouldn't there be a way to deal with them in this world? The police and the courts, of course. That's why they existed. If they weren't working, how could you trigger them into action?

Father Ed's blue Chevy rolled down the county road while Jason ruminated. A few minutes later, his condolences expressed, Father Ed asked, "To your knowledge, was your father under undue pressure? Was there anything going on that would cause him to take such a drastic step?"

Jason gazed at the priest in silence.

"My apologies if I'm being insensitive, Jason. I don't mean to offend. I've already discussed this with your mother, but I'm very concerned with your well-being. Severe stress can alleviate or diminish a person's responsibility for taking his own life."

Jason nodded inwardly. He had guessed right about the reason for Father Ed's visit.

"He was really depressed, Father. It started when that man died at the paper company. My dad started drinking a lot. He and my mom weren't getting along."

"How so?"

"Well, they argued quite a bit, and Dad slept in our spare bedroom."

"I see." The priest gazed into the distance. "By the way, where's Luke?" He reached into his pocket. "I have a treat for him."

"Someone killed Luke. Dad thought it was his fault for leaving Luke outside while we were gone."

"My gosh! What did they do, poison him?"

"They cut him in half."

"Good Lord, Jason! When did this happen?"

"Fourth of July. Remember when my dad choked on the communion bread? That happened the day after we found Luke dead. I think my dad thought God was calling him."

Closing his eyes and shaking his head, Father Ed took a deep breath. "I'm so sorry, Jason. I had no idea your father was going through such a difficult period." He draped his arm over Jason's shoulders. "Anything else? I mean, what happened to Luke was horrendous, no question. However, for your wonderful father to take his life, well…"

"Father, I don't know my dad's thoughts. I told you how hard he took it over his friend who died at work. And he and my mom were fighting an awful lot. I think it got to be too much for him. I think what happened to Luke broke his heart and his spirit."

The priest nodded, but didn't look convinced. "Let's pray," he said.

They said a Hail Mary, an Our Father, and a Glory Be

together before the priest departed.

Jason's thoughts remained on his dad, whose body lay at the mortuary. Where was he, actually? He was in heaven and that was so far away.

Although Jason had left some things out, everything he had told Father Ed was true. He would have lied if necessary in order to make sure his father received a Requiem Mass and burial in consecrated ground. His dad was a good man. God knew that, and God knew why he had taken his life.

White billowy clouds floated overhead against a cornflower-blue sky, not the type of day Jason associated with funerals. Nothing seemed to conform to his notions of life anymore. Father Ed, his black Rite of Committal book in hand, presided at the head of the closed casket poised over the gaping hole beneath the artificial turf and floral displays.

"Because God has chosen to call our brother from this life to himself, we commit his body to the earth, for we are dust and unto dust we shall return. But the Lord Jesus will change our mortal bodies to be like His in glory, for He is risen, the firstborn of the dead. So let us commend our brother Michael to the Lord that He may embrace him in peace and raise up his body on the last day."

Most of the three or four dozen people at the graveside ritual said Amen. Jason and his mother each placed a rose on the coffin. Father Ed held Linda's hands in his while he said a few words to her that Jason only half-heard.

The priest shook hands with Jason. "Your father was a good man, Jason. A good, honest man who loved his family and lived his faith. Someday everything will be revealed to us, and you will see him again. I know you'll be strong. For yourself and for your mother."

People drifted away to their cars. Marvin Pell stood off to the side near the funeral director for a few minutes before he, too, sauntered off.

"I'll see you in a few minutes," Father Ed said as he left. Only the two of them and the funeral director remained. Dark clouds that had piled up in the west earlier now moved in with a quickening breeze that chilled the air and carried the scent of rain.

"Let's go, Mom. Lunch is in the parish hall."

She turned to him slowly with a strange look in her eyes, a piercing yet vacant expression that scared him.

"Your father doesn't want me to leave. He wants me to stay here with him."

"Come on, Mom. We have to go. We'll bake out here in this sun."

"Yes, we don't want to bake. We're not cakes. Oh, I have the granddaddy of headaches! That's why muffins split on top. The baking gives them splitting headaches!"

She laughed in a high-pitched, shrill way devoid of mirth. The funeral director looked the other way.

"It's only a little way to the car, Mom."

He led his mother to the black hearse as large raindrops began to pelt them.

A warm sunny afternoon followed the brief morning storm. At sundown, Jason rode his bike to the cemetery. Standing at his father's grave and facing into the sunset, with tears running down his face, he played "Taps" on his father's bugle. His father had also taught him the lyrics.

> *Day is done, gone the sun*
> *From the lakes, from the hills, from the sky*
> *All is well, safely at rest*
> *God is near.*
>
> *Fading light dims the sight*
> *And a star gems the sky, gleaming bright*
> *From afar, drawing near*
> *Falls the night.*
> *Thanks and praise for our days*
> *Neath the sun, neath the stars, neath the sky*
> *As we go, this we know*
> *God is near.*

The last plaintive note died away. When Jason lowered the bugle and said, "Goodbye, Dad," his resolve not to cry left him. He fell to the ground, spread-eagled over his father's grave. His fingers dug into the moist sod, and he cried harder than he had ever cried in his life.

Minutes later, numb and drained of tears, he lay without movement until the dampness of the fresh grave chilled him and the soil muddied his clothes. Hungry for the first time since his father died, he straddled his bike and pedaled down the shadowy gravel road of Calvary Cemetery. It was getting late. His mom would be worried about him.

Chapter Fifteen

In the past, if Father Ed happened to driving by, he would sometimes stop in for a cup of coffee and maybe play catch with Jason or challenge him to a quick match of catechism trivia, a game they had concocted a year or so ago.

The game revolved around Church teachings. They took turns asking each other questions that had to be answered fully and with supporting evidence. Father Ed always won, but Jason had closed the gap by doing a lot of research. He enjoyed the study and figured it would help him some day in seminary.

Father Ed stopped by more frequently since the funeral, which Jason appreciated. Today he spoke privately with Linda for a few minutes before coming out to the porch where Jason sat with a pair of binoculars hanging from his neck.

Jason had heard enough of the conversation to know that it concerned a job with Mr. Bensen, the custodian at Augustine High, for the remainder of the summer. A good guy with a wonderful sense of humor and an infectious laugh, Mr. Bensen was popular with students and faculty alike.

Jason had also heard enough to realize his mother didn't seem to care one way or another if he took the job. Her apathy surprised him and yet it didn't. They could sure use the money, but she had been acting more and more strangely ever since the funeral. She seemed distracted all the time and didn't show much interest in anything, including food. She prepared Jason's meals but ate very little herself, even less than before.

"What would I do, Father?"

"Mostly cut grass at the school and Calvary Cemetery. The school needs cleaning, floors need waxing. The pay is two dollars an hour."

"I'll do it. When do I start?"

"Come to the school at seven tomorrow morning, dressed for work."

"Okay. Right now I have to bike into town."

"Want a lift? I'm going that way."

"No thanks, Father. I'm going to bike it."

He straddled his bicycle and headed for the driveway.

Jason leaned his bike against a utility pole in front of the post office. Inside, only one other person, a woman about his mother's age, stood in line at the counter. Her pale flesh bulged in every direction from her too-tight black shorts. Jason knew his mother would never wear anything like that if she weighed that much. The woman finally finished mailing a package.

"Need any stamps today?" the postal clerk asked her as she turned to go.

"No, thanks."

Jason approached the counter. "I have to deliver something, but I lost the directions. Can you help me?"

"Sure try. Name?"

Jason glanced at a slip of paper in his hand. "Mr. Virgil Badeen and Mr. William Sinkhorn."

"Spelling on Badeen?"

"B-a-d-e-e-n."

"Just a sec." The clerk twice spun a large circular contraption that was mounted on a heavy wire frame. He ran his finger down a column of white labels encased in plastic. "Route two. Here's the fire number. It's on Creamery Drive. I'd say just east of Richland Crick. What's that second name again?"

"Sinkhorn."

The clerk spun the device again. "Sinkhorn. Route three. West of the crick just south of where Badeen lives. Creamery Drive separates the routes," he said with a chuckle that mystified Jason, and wrote the information on the paper and slid it across the counter.

"Thank you."

"Don't forget, it's against the law to put anything in a mailbox. You can mail something or hand it to them, but you can't put it in their mail box."

"I won't."

Jason knew the whereabouts of Creamery Drive. The old cheese factory about four miles from the Ferris home had closed a long time ago. Someone still occupied the house connected to the factory.

Thick woods flanked the asphalt county road where it intersected Creamery Drive, a gravel road. Small stones pinged against his bike frame when Jason turned onto the gravel and peddled until he saw a mailbox next to a rutted driveway. No name showed on the mailbox, only a number that matched the number the postal clerk had given him. The dense timber standing beyond the mailbox obstructed his view of a barely visible white house a hundred yards from the road.

Jason pedaled farther down the road before veering into the ditch. He swung off his bike, walked the bike into the trees, and laid it in the weeds. Then he picked his way on foot deeper into the woods.

Circling around the white house, he found a hiding spot across a pond from the building he had seen from the mailbox. He crawled into a cluster of alders and ferns. The pond was only about a hundred feet wide, so he didn't need the binoculars. He focused them anyway.

The house nestled in a clearing littered by a stack of old tires, a rusted automobile, a turned-over washing machine, and various other junk. An ax, its blade imbedded in a chopping block, angled up near two rows of stacked firewood. Paint peeled on the house.

Badeen, shirtless, sat on a large block of wood drinking a beer from an open twelve-pack at his side. He looked like a football player. Jason had never seen shoulders, arms, and legs so massive and muscular as Badeen's.

A square-gripped pistol protruded from a holster on his right hip. A small white dog perched on his lap, and a dark brown Doberman lay at his feet next to a red cooler. Jason dropped the binoculars away from his eyes in order to increase his field of vision. He quietly snapped on the lens caps and resumed watching the scene across the pond.

Badeen drained his beer and tossed the empty can into the pond. As if on cue, the lap dog jumped to the ground. The Doberman rolled to its feet with a growl. Badeen sprang up and drew the pistol in one motion. He fired one shot into the can. Water spouted five feet into the air. The bullet-ripped can sank.

After re-holstering his pistol, Badeen ambled up a dirt path to an outhouse not far from his home. With his back to Jason, he urinated without closing the door, zipped up, and returned to the woodpile. His muscles rippled when he yanked the ax from the chopping block.

Jason's teeth prickled as he observed Badeen. He looked as dangerous as Jason knew him to be. As much as Jason hated him, he couldn't stop watching him splitting the wood with powerful, single blows. The pond separated them and Jason felt the sensation of danger without actually being in danger.

Oddly enough, Badeen conjured up an image of a man-eating komodo dragon—vicious, mesmerizing, and vile. After watching the man for thirty minutes, Jason quietly retreated from his hiding spot.

Retrieving his bike, he sped down the road and found Sinkhorn's mailbox. He hid his bike among the trees and found his way to a hiding place across a creek from Sinkhorn's home.

Unlike Badeen's messy place, Sinkhorn's was neat and even had flowerbeds. His pink house looked freshly painted. A black Lab, obviously carrying a litter in her belly, lay on her side beneath a mature pin oak tree. A purple Harley leaned on its kickstand at the corner of the detached garage.

When the screen door of the house flew open, Jason winced and scraped his head on a branch. He ducked down, fearful that Sinkhorn had heard the noise, but the man gave no indication that he had. The sun gleamed on his bald head when he stepped off the small stoop. The dog waddled up to him for an ear scratch before Sinkhorn mounted his Harley and roared off.

Jason retraced the route he had taken into the woods. How could two relatively ordinary-looking men be killers? What could possibly turn them into that? Their upbringing? Their genes? Both? If God made human beings in his image, why would He allow some of them to turn into monsters?

He would have to read Saint Augustine again and maybe some others. Things just didn't add up.

Chapter Sixteen

Jason found his mother lying on the sofa with a wet washrag across her forehead.

"Hi, honey. Where've you been all afternoon?"

"Just hanging out."

"That was nice of Father Ed to line up that job for you. The money will come in handy."

"Sure will."

"I don't know what we're going to do. Your dad had some life insurance at work and a little bit he bought on his own. If they pay, it won't last long. I'll have to find a job." She adjusted the washrag that had slipped to the side.

"What do you mean, 'if they pay'? You think maybe they won't?"

"Honey, they couldn't stay in business very long if people bought life insurance and then…."

"Oh."

"I need a couple of aspirin. Will you get them for me?"

"Sure, Mom."

Backtracking to the kitchen, he half-filled a glass of water before shaking the last two aspirin into his hand. He lifted the lid of the trash basket to dispose of the container and noticed his mother's medicine lying on top of the garbage. He reclaimed the nearly full plastic bottle.

Why would she discard her medication? He returned to the living room.

"Here, Mom." He handed her the aspirin and water.

"I don't need the water, honey. Thanks."

Jason held up the bottle of prescription drugs. "Why'd you throw this out, Mom? You have to take this stuff."

"Oh, it must have fallen into the garbage by mistake."

"How? It couldn't have."

"Well, I don't need it anymore, anyway."

"Yes, you do. You know you do."

"Don't sass me!"

"Mom, you can't just give up. Please take your medicine the way you're supposed to."

"If you think you can stand there and order me around, you're wrong. Now stop or get out!" She chewed the aspirin and turned away from him. He bent over her and hugged her. He found her hand and squeezed it.

"We'll be okay, Mom. We'll be okay."

"I'm so glad, honey, that you'll be a priest and won't have to work in some nasty factory. I'll be so proud of you."

He hugged her again. "I'll be happy that you're proud of me, Mom. You'd better rest now."

He stood upright. His dad was gone. Was his mom slipping away, too? A shiver coursed through him. After staring at his mother for a few moments, he left the house and got on his bike again. He had to make another trip into town.

That night Jason hunched over a plat map marked with two squares, one identified with a capital B, the other with a capital S. A diagonal line connected the two squares.

Less than a mile apart through the woods, and the same creek runs through both of their properties.

He folded the map and stuck it into the middle drawer of his desk before he undressed and climbed into bed.

He had no idea how long he had been asleep when the sound of someone singing awakened him.

> *He walks with me/*
> *And He talks with me/*
> *And He tells me I am his own.*

Instantly wide-awake but disoriented, he recognized his mother's voice coming from outside.

> *And the joy we share/*
> *As we tarry there.*

The alarm clock on the nightstand glowed two a.m. Jason bolted upright. He rolled out of bed, squirmed into his pants, took the steps three at a time, and raced into the yard. His mother, her arms extended, swayed gracefully on the grass in her nightgown, as if in a reverie.

"Mom," he said gently.

"Oh! You scared me."

"Let's go inside, Mom."

"I like it here."

"Aren't you cold?"

"Not with your father here."

Jason took a deep breath and held his arm out to her. "Dad wouldn't want you to catch pneumonia."

She stopped in mid-motion and stood like a statue for a second or two before twirling around, a dreamy look on her face. "Maybe I could be with him always."

"Would you want me to be alone?"

His mother frowned. Then her face softened. Taking Jason's hand, she allowed him to lead her to the house.

Chapter Seventeen

It had to be the hottest day of the year. No breeze blew through the old part of Calvary Cemetery where Jason pushed a power mower around and between the large monuments—some of them tilted, others sunken or crumbling, most of them in one stage or another of decay.

Sweat rolled off his bare upper body, and grass clippings stuck to his legs below his shorts. He liked the sweet smell of cut grass that mingled with the exhaust of the mower. He wore one of his father's sweat-stained LaFarge Paper caps. His earphones, connected to a Walkman at his waist, blasted out Led Zeppelin.

Before he had begun mowing, he had trimmed around each monument with a weed trimmer. The new section of the cemetery, where his dad was buried, was much easier to mow. The headstones there lay flush with the ground so the mower rolled right over them and no trimming was necessary.

A blue Chevy turned off Stephens Street and crept down the gravel road, stopping near Jason. Father Ed swung his legs out from under the steering wheel and joined Jason near a tall gravestone marking the plot of someone who had died in 1941. Jason turned off the mower and the Walkman.

"Mr. Bensen says you're a hard worker. Thanks for making me look good." The priest wiped his face with a white handkerchief. "It's been a terrible summer, Jason. I know it's still too soon, but is it getting any better for you? You okay?"

"Mr. Bensen's a good boss. The money will sure help too. My mom doesn't think my dad's life insurance will pay."

"I've checked into that, and it's okay. After two years, they have to pay no matter how a person died."

Father Ed seemed intent on reading the tombstone to his

left. "He does a beautiful job out here. Makes Calvary the best-kept cemetery around. He takes pride."

Jason brushed grass from the mower and wiped his hands.

"Of course, Jason, crab grass and weeds always manage to get in. It's mostly good grass though. More good than bad, by far."

"Easier to get rid of weeds than a lot of other things, Father."

"Isn't a weed just a different kind of grass?"

Squinting against the sun, Jason contemplated the priest. "Do you believe there's any comparison between grass and bull thistles? Ever wonder why God created thistles?"

"Don't you think an ecologist could give us any number of reasons?"

"What good are they?"

"How can we know?"

"They serve no good purpose."

"How can you be so sure?"

Jason leaned against the stone of the man who had died in 1941.

"Some things you just know. Do you like snakes, Father?"

"No. They scare the daylights out of me."

"Me, too. But I can't help watching them. Then I have nightmares. I mean, real nightmares."

"Are you praying every day?"

"More than ever." He swept his hand across the sweat on his forehead. "Doesn't seem to be working."

"We need to pray for the right things. No, not right things. We need to pray right. For guidance and strength. In a word, for grace."

"Father, why do we have venomous snakes? Non-poisonous snakes survive just fine. Did you know that possums are immune to snake venom? Over time the snakes' venom gets stronger. Did God create such evolutionary variety for His entertainment?

"Why does the entire system of nature depend on death? I mean painful death. Sometimes at night I hear the most awful, pitiful cries of animals being attacked and eaten alive. Why is there so much pain in our world?"

Father Ed again appeared to study the 1941 tombstone before answering. "I don't know that I can give you any reason other than to look to the cross."

A thorn of anger pricked Jason. He looked away from the priest.

"Let me quote Stott, a British clergyman: 'In the real world of pain, how could one worship a God who was immune to it?' Point is, there must be a reason for pain, a reason we can't see, because our God suffered horrific pain on the cross and in the events leading up to the cross. Why else would he do that? Dying on the cross wasn't necessary. He could have redeemed us with a wave of his hand."

"What about those who cause pain? You've got to be evil to intentionally make others suffer. Why would God permit such evil to exist if he loves us?"

Father Ed seemed engrossed in the 1941 marker.

"As we've discussed before, evil is the absence of good, as darkness is the absence of light. You know from your catechism that evil stems from our free will. Let's consider the bright side. Many virtues would not exist without evil. Things like heroism, mercy, forgiveness, and perseverance. Take courage, for example. Courage would be impossible without the danger of physical or mental pain."

Father Ed rested his hand on Jason's shoulder.

"I know you're a big Cubs fan. When a batter gets in the box, he's hoping for a hit, maybe even a homerun. But he might strike out. Striking out, or the possibility of it, makes getting a hit rewarding. What fun—or virtue, if you will—would there be in hitting a homerun every time?"

"I guess analogies help up to a point."

Father Ed tugged at the sleeve of his shirt and seemed a little distracted. "Are you worried about your father, Jason?"

"What do you mean?"

"Well, going back to our earlier conversation, he apparently took his own life. However, based on what you told me, you shouldn't have cause to worry about his soul."

"I'm not worried about my father's soul. I just miss him. I'd like to ask you a hypothetical question, Father."

"Fire away."

"What if someone committed suicide to protect someone else? Is that justified?"

"It sounds on its face like the end justifying the means. So my first inclination would be to say no, it's not justified."

"Soldiers receive medals for giving up their lives to save other soldiers. I read about a marine who fell on a live grenade to save his buddies. He received the Medal of Honor. That is, his parents did."

"That soldier's primary motivation wasn't the loss of his own life. Rather, he sacrificed his life to save those around him."

"So the end did justify the means."

"The grenade probably would have killed the entire group. One man sacrificed his life to spare others. A truly heroic, unpremeditated act."

"Does premeditation make a difference, Father?"

"Well, it could, don't you think? If a person has time to think it through and decides that suicide, even to protect others, is the way to go, then he freely chooses death over all other options. In all likelihood, a better resolution exists. Suicide could well be an escape from unpleasantness or embarrassment. That would be cowardly and an affront to God."

"Isn't that what Christ did, gave up his life for the rest of us? Wasn't that a form of premeditated suicide?"

A troubled expression crossed Father Ed's face, followed by a furrowed brow. "Did you read that?"

"No. I thought about it recently."

"Another mystery in God's plan for us. I'm not sure we're talking about equivalent issues—"

"But we are, Father. This has nothing to do with my dad. His death got me thinking, though, and this is one of the questions I have. Christ's death was a premeditated suicide to save humanity. Why would a similar motive in a human being be less valid if Christ is our model?"

"I'd have to have more information and think it through."

Jason grabbed the handle of the lawn mower. "I'd better get back to work, Father. I have to finish this whole section by quitting time." He bent over and pulled the cord on the mower. The machine howled to life with a deafening roar that drowned out any words the priest may have uttered.

Left hanging, Father Ed started to leave. He half-turned to face Jason. "Keep up the good work," he shouted over the mower. "Remember, it's faith *and* good works."

Was he serious or making a joke? Jason waved goodbye and resumed mowing.

He would not talk to Father Ed about the murder his dad had seen.

Chapter Eighteen

After numerous trips through the woods to observe Badeen and Sinkhorn at their homes, Jason knew their routines and habits. He also knew how to get from one house to the other so well that he could have found his way in the dark.

He didn't really know why he spied on the two men. What good could it do? And it could get dangerous. They were killers, after all. But no matter how many times he questioned his motives, he couldn't stay away. They repulsed and attracted him with a power that defied logic.

How could they kill a man the way they had killed Mr. Walker? And once they had done it, how could they not be consumed by guilt? Could the same God that created normal people have created them? How could their consciences have formed so differently from those of most people?

He wished they would die … better yet, that he could kill them. The consequences made him shudder. A failed attempt would probably result in his own death. If he succeeded and got caught, he would spend years in prison. His dad had been right when he refused Mr. Pell's suggestion that they kill Badeen and Sinkhorn. But what if he somehow succeeded in killing them and got away with it? What would that be like?

Jason's heart beat faster every time he approached his hiding places, usually wearing a Green Bay Packer T-shirt because the color blended so well the trees and undergrowth. Today was no different.

His heart pounded and his temples pulsed as he slipped into the cluster of alders across the pond from Badeen's home. The Doberman lay in the shade of a short sugar maple near the pond. Badeen's pickup was parked on the gravel driveway.

Jason's heart rate was slowing to normal when Badeen's

door opened and the little white lapdog scampered out. Badeen followed the dog, the black pistol riding on his right hip as usual. Only thing different, he had some kind of large pad on his left arm.

The Doberman immediately leaped to its feet. Tail wagging, the dog pranced and wiggled as Badeen approached and began circling him. The Doberman crouched low in a springing position and concentrated on his master's movements. The lapdog barked nonstop.

Badeen leaned forward and slapped the padding with his right hand. "Attack!"

The Doberman bared its teeth and lunged at Badeen with a deep-throated growl. Badeen thrust the padded arm at the dog's gaping mouth. The dog's teeth sank into the padding. Badeen twisted and turned in an effort to shake the dog loose. If not for the padding, the dog would have shredded Badeen's arm. The lapdog ran about, yapping even more excitedly than before.

"Halt!"

The Doberman released Badeen's arm. Badeen reached into his pocket and extracted what looked like a large milk bone.

"Sit!"

The dog immediately squatted on its haunches to receive the treat. While the Doberman wolfed it down, Badeen extended a smaller treat to the lapdog. With his immense hands, he scraped up five empty beer cans from the chopping block, tossed them into the pond, and drew his pistol. Five rapid rounds sank all five cans.

Badeen reloaded the clip and shoved the pistol into the holster, scooped up the lapdog, and cradled it against his chest. The roar of a motorcycle told Jason it was eight-thirty. Sinkhorn arrived at Badeen's place every Sunday morning at the same time.

Sinkhorn rolled down the gravel driveway on his purple Harley. He stopped between Badeen and the house and revved his motor. Neither man said a word. Badeen, still holding the small dog, headed for the house. Sinkhorn turned off the

Harley, rocked it onto the kickstand, and followed Badeen inside.

Jason, his heart beating harder than ever, glanced at his watch and tore off into the woods at an angle away from the road where he had ditched his bike. He knew exactly how long it would take him to get to Sinkhorn's place. He always timed it anyway.

Chapter Nineteen

Jason and Larry McGraw stood side by side with folded hands as Father Ed elevated the host and chalice.

"This is the Lamb of God," Father Ed intoned, "who takes away the sins of the world. Happy are those who are called to his supper."

Everyone in the church responded, "Lord, I am not worthy to receive you, but only say the word and I shall be healed."

The boys cupped their hands to receive the host.

"The Body of Christ," Father Ed said as he placed the host in their palms.

"Amen."

They proceeded to the small bench to the left of the altar and sat motionless while Father Ed and the lay ministers distributed communion. Jason began his habit of counting the number of people who received only the host versus how many received the host and the wine.

He personally never drank the wine after others had drunk from the same chalice. As meaningful as it might be to receive under both species, the same way the apostles did at the Last Supper, the physical act of doing so disgusted him. Some people drooled, and others looked so unappetizing that he wouldn't want to sit at the same table with them, let alone share cups or glasses. His attitude carried some reproach with it, but not enough to make him change his mind.

Aside from receiving the Body of Christ through the host, serving at mass excited him in a quiet way and filled him with wonder, unlike the excitement he felt when he was with Cari or thinking about her, an excitement so much more intense and physical.

He yearned for the day of his ordination and the ability to consecrate the bread and wine as Jesus had at the last supper.

The Cari excitement generated guilt and made him want to get to confession right away. Why then did thoughts of Cari always overtake him? Why were they so powerful and awesome and wondrous?

His daydreaming ceased. Not thirty feet from him, Billy Sinkhorn stood in line to receive communion. All cleaned up, dressed in a light blue shirt and navy slacks, he cupped his hands for the host, laid it on his tongue, crossed himself, and pivoted to return to his pew.

The altar, the people, the entire church swirled. Only Sinkhorn's shaved head stayed in focus as it moved away into the far reaches of the church. Everything else blurred. Jason gulped for air and felt sweat on his forehead and in his armpits. He closed his eyes to stop the swirling sensation. Anger choked his throat.

You can't kill someone and receive communion! What's going on?

The remaining communicants shuffled forward to receive the Eucharist as Jason watched Sinkhorn leave.

Had Sinkhorn confessed and been absolved? What kind of priest would do that? Everything was crazy. Crazy and just plain awful.

"Jason? Psssst! Jason! Wake up!"

Communion over, Father Ed was trying to get Jason's attention to conclude mass. Jason snapped to attention and managed to find his way through the closing rites.

Later in the sacristy, he and Larry helped Father Ed with the task of storing the vestments.

"Hey, Larry," Jason said, "you can take off. I'll help Father stash this stuff."

"All right! See you later, dude."

"And this is for the handshake." He punched Larry's shoulder hard. Larry laughed and slipped out the door. Larry had given him a bone-crunching sign of peace following the Lord's Prayer.

After Larry's departure, Jason folded his surplice and laid

it on a shelf.

"You fell asleep on the job, Ferris. I thought I'd have to throw holy water in your face to get your attention."

"Yeah, sorry, Father."

"How's your mother doing?"

Jason shrugged. "She seems awfully forgetful, like her mind is somewhere else most of the time. I'm afraid she doesn't care much about anything anymore."

"Be more patient with her than ever before, Jason. She may need a year or more to get over her grief."

"Father, what would you do if someone confessed a serious crime?"

"What kind of crime? How serious?"

"Could you forgive murder?"

"Under Canon law, I can forgive someone who has killed."

"And that would be the end of it? What about penance?"

"Let's start with defining murder. Premeditated murder is different from someone getting killed in a bar fight, for example. Circumstances would come into play. Was there an element of self-defense? Does the perpetrator have a family for me to consider? What's his track record?

"A case like that would probably take more than one session. I'd have to be certain the person had repented and was deeply and sincerely sorry. And I would have to consider the consequences of his act. For example, did the victim leave a family that would be destitute with him gone?

"That's not to say an upstanding citizen's life is more valuable or less valuable than, say, a homeless person's, but the consequences would be different in each case. Everything would have to be taken into account."

"Let's say it was premeditated and the victim left a family behind."

"What's this all about, Jason?"

"I'm curious. What if someone confesses a murder to me after I'm a priest?"

"Don't worry. Your seminary training will equip you."

"What would you do if someone confessed he had killed

someone in cold blood?"

"Here, help me with this. I always end up dragging it on the floor."

Jason grabbed the bottom of the vestment. They folded it and hung it in a closet.

"Whether I knew the person or not, I would insist on a face-to-face meeting. I'd have to know every detail, and I'd want to look into his eyes when he told me. I would probably consult with the bishop. I might or might not extend absolution. Either way, I would in all likelihood urge him to go to the authorities, depending on the circumstances.

"Don't forget, criminal transgressions are Caesar's bailiwick too. If a murderer deserved to be punished by the state, I'd insist that he turn himself in as a condition for absolution."

"A confession like that must really be tough on the priest."

"I've never had one, hope I never do. That would be a killer, no pun intended."

So Sinkhorn had not confessed to Father Ed. Had he gone somewhere else and confessed to another priest? Probably not. A man willing to destroy another human being wouldn't get hung up on the rules of the Church, any more than he would on secular laws. To receive communion with the stain of murder on your soul was unforgivable.

Chapter Twenty

Jason lay on his bed too keyed up to sleep. The scent of cut alfalfa wafted into the room on a cool west breeze that ruffled the curtains. The glow of a full moon poured through the window along with the sounds of night creatures, many of which would not survive until dawn. Eat or be eaten, kill or be killed, the eternal cycle of Nature.

Two men had caused three deaths—one of the men was so depraved that he may well have received communion with murder on his conscience. There had to be exceptions to the Church's rule against hating anyone.

A fine line divided anger and hate. Which came first? Or could it go either way, depending on the circumstances? He didn't know the answer. He did know he hated two people.

A female voice drifted into the bedroom. Jason listened intently for a moment before leaping from bed and hastening to the north window at the end of the hallway. The garage light and moonlight provided scant illumination, just enough to reveal his mother at the edge of the road. She was naked.

"…and after the ball game we'll go to a fancy hotel and pretend we're in high society. Won't that be fun?"

Jason yanked a blanket from his bed and hurtled down the stairs three at a time in his T-shirt and boxer shorts. He broad jumped off the porch and shot across the wet grass. In the middle of the road, his mother, a dreamy, distant expression on her face, whirled in slow circles.

> *Take me out to the ball game/*
> *Take me out with the crowd/*
> *Buy me some—*

"Mom!"

She froze in position and stopped singing. Jason rushed to her side, holding out the blanket.

"What do you want?"

"Come inside, Mom. Please?"

"Your father's with me."

He threw the blanket over her and gently took her by the wrist. "You've got to get off the road. It's dangerous."

She yanked her arm free and backed away in a crouch. The blanket fell to the pavement.

"Don't tell me what to do! You think you can order me around? Maybe you don't like girls? That why you want to be a priest?"

"Mom! For crying out loud!"

"Ever seen a naked girl?"

Tears ran down his face. Lights flashed on at Cari's house. Jason ran inside to the phone.

Jason didn't know if the doctor behind the desk had grandkids, but he sure looked like a grandfather ought to look. Both of Jason's grandfathers had died. One grandmother had remarried and moved to Florida. The other one, on his mother's side, lived only fifty miles away but had never spoken to Jason's father when he was alive. She still wouldn't talk to her daughter because she had married Michael Ferris, although Jason never knew why.

Father Ed sat next to Jason across from the doctor.

"She needs to go away for a rest," the doctor said.

Jason looked at Father Ed.

"She has to get her strength back," Father Ed said. "It's been a terrible time for her. For both of you."

"Just so she's taken care of."

"Do you have relatives nearby?" the doctor asked.

"Our next door neighbors said I can stay with them for a while. Will she get better? Please tell me the truth."

The doctor hesitated and glanced at the priest. "It's too early to say, son. All we can do is hope for the best. Your mother will receive excellent care."

"What exactly happened?"

The doctor brushed something invisible off the left sleeve of his navy sport coat. "Your mother has had a severe mental breakdown, son. She simply can't process information—that is, sensory data—and organize it within the context of her day-to-day activities.

"As you know, she's had a history of certain issues, and she's no doubt been under tremendous strain following the passing of your father. Such a time is difficult for anyone, let alone those with a fragile constitution. Quite often rest and therapy enable patients to regroup. In your mother's case, we won't know for several months at the earliest."

Father Ed laid his arm over Jason's shoulders. "We'll pray for her to progress and come home soon, Jason."

"Okay, Father. Thank you, doctor, for being honest with me."

Chapter Twenty-One

The weather turned cold and wet on a Friday night. Howling winds transformed the rain into horizontal pellets. The rain moderated to intermittent showers on Saturday and became a steady downpour for most of Sunday.

Jason used the time to reread Dante's *Inferno*. He told the Langs he had plenty of food at home and would be fine for a while. The hellish weather and lack of distractions probably added more impact to the *Inferno* than it otherwise would have had. Even allowing for those factors, Jason found the book just as intriguing, ingenious, and terrifying as he had the first time he'd read it a year ago.

The outer ring of the Seventh Circle, the place reserved for murderers and others guilty of violent acts, transfixed him. Sinners condemned to this location for eternity found themselves immersed to varying depths in a river of boiling blood and fire, guarded by Centaurs. Any sinner who sought relief from the pain of burning blood by rising up higher than allowed immediately received an arrow from the bow of a Centaur and would collapse into the hot blood for even more excruciating pain.

Would boiling blood be sticky and cling to the flesh? It would certainly cause scalding, so the victims would blister from head to foot. Or would their flesh peel away from their bones to expose the innards to the hotness and then become whole again to repeat the process forever?

A fitting place for Badeen and Sinkhorn. A perversely delicious thought to dwell on, yet Jason felt a twinge of guilt for wishing that kind of punishment on anyone—Father Ed surely wouldn't approve—so he alternated between imagining them in boiling blood and saying Hail Marys as a sort of penance. His heart wasn't in the Hail Marys.

Whenever he tired of reading, he poured himself another glass of Kool-Aid and roamed around the house. So quiet and gloomy, more like a cave or detention cell, the empty house depressed him, especially at night when it got scary. He invariably found himself at a west window peering through the rain at the Lang house hoping to catch a glimpse of Cari.

He tried not to think of his mother in that God-forsaken place they had taken her to. He had not gone inside. He had waited in Father Ed's car while the paramedics and the priest escorted her into the building. Selfish and cowardly behavior, he knew, but the outside of the institutional-looking structure looked foreboding enough. He didn't want to see where his mother would spend her time, did not want that scene imbedded in his memory.

Surrounded by the awful weather, haunted by thoughts of his mother and visions of the *Inferno*, Jason found in Cari his only sunny image: the way she kidded him, chided him, laughed, acted at times like a drama queen; the way she smiled, the way her lustrous wavy hair fell nearly to her shoulders, the way her butt jiggled when she walked, the way her breasts jutted against her blouses and shirts. His knees got shaky when she wore a T-shirt, or, no matter what she wore, if her nipples showed.

Just a word from her could taunt his imagination for days. Once, on a cold autumn day, she had laughingly said, "It's a nippley kind of day!" He had dwelled on her words for weeks, knowing he would remember them and her tone of voice until his last breath, and would always associate the incident with chilly autumn days. How could a girl be so offhandedly funny and smart and seductive at the same time?

He envisioned himself in the second circle of the *Inferno*, the place reserved for people who had allowed lust to overcome them during their lives. Compared with the deeper circles of hell, mild punishment awaited sinners banished to the second circle. Here, strong winds blew illicit lovers and others helter-skelter with no respite or hope for calm.

How appropriate, he decided, because when you started

thinking about a girl, she was all you could think about, and the thoughts wouldn't let you alone until you found release or something else came along to distract you momentarily—and without question, the distraction was always momentary.

The sun finally reappeared in a diluted blue sky with temperatures and humidity in the mid-nineties. Everything stayed wet and spongy for another couple days. Jason and Mr. Bensen could not mow grass, so they worked inside the high school, scrubbing and waxing the floors.

Jason and the Langs had agreed that he would sleep in his own house, prepare his own breakfast and lunch, but eat dinner with them on most days. He would have preferred eating all meals at home. Mrs. Lang insisted, however, that he "eat at least one good meal a day."

There was a delay in receiving the life insurance because the insurance companies said they couldn't pay the money to his mother while she was hospitalized. The courts had to name a guardian for Jason, and other issues had to be settled. He wasn't sure how it all worked. For the time being they would all take it one day at a time and make it work.

The recent rains had swollen the creek that ran through Sinkhorn's property. The rippling sounds of its swift current reached Jason as he crouched in his usual surveillance location.

Just as he enjoyed reading and watching television documentaries on Hitler and the Nazis, in spite of the disgust he felt over their slaughter of millions, he could not stop watching Badeen and Sinkhorn from the safety of his hiding places. Did the evil they represented attract him? Did he have a latent longing for the dark side? He wondered and worried about those things yet couldn't stay away.

Today, the black Lab lay on her side crowded by a writhing litter of newborn pups. Sinkhorn appeared in his doorway. He sauntered over to the dogs. After hovering over them for a minute or so, he wheeled around and strode to his garage. He returned carrying a medium-size cardboard box, which he set on the ground near the dogs. One by one he dropped all the pups into the box while the mother frantically circled him, whining and yipping and barking.

After folding the flaps shut, Sinkhorn carried the box to the edge of the creek and heaved it into the water where it floated downstream on a swift current. Sinkhorn watched it for a few moments before heading back to the house. The black Lab plunged into the water, desperately, hopelessly trying to save her babies.

Jason crawled from his hiding place. Keeping an eye on Sinkhorn, he ran headlong through the trees and thick brush to overtake the box.

Sinkhorn turned around. Jason flopped to the ground among the weeds. Sinkhorn kept staring his way. Had he spotted Jason? Jason squinted between the weeds. The box bobbed and turned with the current as it swung into a bend. Sinkhorn continued looking. At long last, he spat on the ground and headed for his house.

Jason sprang up and broke into a run. He gained a little on the box but not enough. Now out of Sinkhorn's line of sight, he ran faster. Branches slapped and scratched his face. One sharp broken-off branch stabbed his shoulder. The box began to sink as Jason pulled abreast of it.

He plunged into the water and stroked hard. The box had sunk halfway under water. He reached out and got one hand beneath it. Gasping for breath, he held the box above water and angled toward the bank. The current kept him from reaching shore. He lay back, cradled the box on his chest, and floated with the current.

The creek snaked around another bend, a tight one. The current swung him and the box close to shore. He kicked his feet hard and reached out with his left arm to clutch a handful of weeds that trailed into the rain-swollen creek. The weeds pulled out of the wet bank. The tug of the current again carried Jason away from the shoreline.

Twisting, he slid his right hand under the box and chucked it as hard as he could into the thick weeds. Then he swam to shore and dragged himself from the water by grasping the weeds hand over hand.

Crawling back to where he had thrown the soggy box, he opened the cardboard flaps. Seven cold, wet puppies with closed eyes squirmed and squealed in an environment far removed from the warm body of their mother.

Cari stood on her porch as Jason dashed across the yard.

"Cari! I need your help! I'll explain on the way. Grab your bike. Dave's coming, too. I'll tell you my plan when we're all together. Hurry!"

Forty-five minutes later, Dave walked his bike with a flat front tire down the gravel driveway and knocked on Sinkhorn's front door. The door swung open a moment later.

"Could I use your phone, mister? My tire went flat. I need to call my dad to come get me."

Sinkhorn surveyed the situation. His eyes scanned the yard and driveway.

"Sure, kid. You live in town?"

"Yessir."

Sinkhorn's eyes swept across the area in front of his house again. He hesitated before leading Dave inside.

Jason and Cari emerged from the undergrowth near the creek. Cari cradled a blanket in her arms as they cautiously approached the black Lab, who peered at them warily, the hair on her back forming a ridge the length of her spine. While still several feet away from the dog, Cari knelt down to reveal one of the Lab's pups wrapped in the blanket. One sniff, and the mother wagged her tail and whined.

Jason snapped a leash on her collar. "Let's get out of here!"

"What will you do with the puppies?"

Jason stretched his legs out across the top steps of Cari's porch and leaned back on his hands. The moonlight glowed softly on his bugle and Cari's violin.

"Do you think evil is only the absence of good? I've always been taught that, but I'm not sure."

"Jason, you need to lighten up. You know, light a candle instead of complaining about the dark? I mean, what does that have to do with the pups?"

"Do you believe people go to hell?"

Cari sighed. "Your dad's in heaven, your mom needs a little rest, Ferris. I wish you wouldn't worry so much."

"Probably everyone needs some time in purgatory before they enter heaven."

"Well, Methodists don't believe in purgatory. I think your dad's in heaven. Jeez, no wonder your mom needed to get some rest. You'd wear anybody out."

"I miss him so much."

Cari hugged him. "Everything will be okay, Jason." They embraced.

"I'm so glad you're here," he said. "Remember that time I fell off the roof and knocked myself out? The first thing I saw when I came to was your face. I actually thought I'd gone to heaven and you were an angel.

"Sounds stupid, but that's what I thought. When you play the violin, it's so magical I almost believe I *am* in heaven. See what I did with the medallion you gave me?"

He reached under his shirt at the neck and pulled out a chain with the small metal violin Cari had given him.

Cari enveloped his hand in hers. "You'll always have it close to you. Close to your heart. How sweet."

Their eyes met. They leaned into each other and kissed. Cari fell back onto the porch, her arms still around Jason, who continued kissing her while lying across her.

"Cari, are you still out there? It's getting a little late."

"Oh, Jeez!" Cari said.

Jason rolled off her and sat up. Cari remained prone.

"We're on the porch, Mother. Just a while longer, okay?"

"All right. Not too long."

Cari's hand caressed Jason's arm. "Does she have great timing or what? Let's go out in the yard."

"Better not."

"You don't like kissing me."

"Oh, man! Not true. Not even sure I should be a priest."

He could feel her eyes on him. She sat up, rearranged her blouse, and straightened her hair.

"I don't know why you want to be a priest. They don't seem to have much fun."

"I promised, remember? And it's what I've always wanted to do. You know, light one candle? It's important to try to make the world a little better."

Cari rolled onto her side, grabbed her violin, and stood up. Facing Jason, she scraped the bow back and forth over the strings to create scratchy squeals. She stopped abruptly.

"You don't have to be a priest to make the world better! Why can't they be more normal? Our pastor's wife is great. Can't imagine *him* without a wife."

"Wish I could marry *and* be a priest. Can't, but I know I'll always wish you were with me."

"Shouldn't you wait till you're older to decide? I mean, is a little kid's promise forever? Jeez Louise, you're talking about your life!" She ran the bow over the strings in another raspy squawk before leaning her violin against the porch railing.

"It's not just my promise to my mom. I never told anyone, but three years ago this spring I fell into the river. The water was over its banks and, man, talk about frigid. The fast current hauled me a quarter-mile downstream in no time at all. I promised God I'd give my life to him if I lived. Not ten seconds later, I bumped into the submerged limb of a tree that had fallen into the water. I clawed my way to shore. Had to be more than luck."

He turned to Cari and cupped her face in his hands. "You're in my heart and always will be. Right now there are bad things there, too."

"Wish you wouldn't talk so gloomy and scary."

"You don't know how scary."

"You'd better come in now, Cari."

"Mo-omm!"

"It's getting late, dear, and you need to practice."

"Might as well. Nothing going on out here. Goodnight, *Ferris*." She grasped her violin and rushed into the house.

Chapter Twenty-Two

From his hiding place across the pond from Badeen's yard, Jason watched Badeen lift a wheelchair from the bed of his pickup and roll it around to the passenger door. He opened the door to assist an old woman from the cab and placed her gently on the wheelchair.

The Doberman remained content to lie on the grass. The little white dog jumped onto the woman's lap as she giggled with delight.

"Let Gramma kiss her little Tootsie!" She kissed and hugged the dog while Badeen, beaming, pushed the wheelchair to a point near the chopping block.

"Close your eyes, Momma."

His mother closed her eyes. Badeen opened a cooler next to the chopping block and lifted out a half-gallon container of ice cream, along with paper bowls and white plastic spoons. He scooped ice cream into the bowls with a metal spoon.

"Okay, Momma, open those peepers."

"Oh, Tootsie! Look what your daddy brung us! Thank you, sweetie!"

"First bite's on me," Badeen said. He held a spoonful to her mouth.

"Mmmmm! So good and creamy! I haven't had ice cream for months."

The little dog jumped to the ground when the old woman reached for the bowl of ice cream Badeen handed her.

"Don't worry, Tootsie," she said, "Gramma will let you lick the bowl."

A buzzing sensation enveloped Jason. His throat constricted with a frustration that equaled the hate he harbored for Badeen. If his reason for spying on the man was to somehow retaliate for his father's death, the scene before him ruled out the idea. Badeen loved his mother. His mother loved and depended on him. Badeen also had a son. Retribution was out of the question. Jason's chest swelled from his labored breathing. He had to move on. Someone else would have to deal with Badeen.

The Doberman growled. Nose up, head jerking left and right, he sniffed the air, then darted to the edge of the pond and began barking directly at Jason, who flattened himself closer to the ground. Peering between the weeds and alders, he could see Badeen staring across the pond to see why his dog was barking.

"Shut up, Rommel!"

The dog cowered momentarily. Within seconds he resumed barking.

"Rommel!" Badeen clapped his hands and advanced toward the dog. The Doberman whined, ran in a tight circle and lay down facing Jason's hiding place. Badeen leaned over to kiss his mother on the cheek. "You eat your ice cream, Momma. I have to go to the house for a minute."

"Don't be too long, Virgie Boy, or I'll eat yours, too."

Badeen laughed. "You better not, Momma," he said over his shoulder as he strolled toward the house.

When Badeen disappeared into the house, Jason waited several minutes before he belly-crawled away. He didn't want to tangle with a Doberman.

As soon as he got far enough away to be completely out of sight, he got to his feet and threaded his way through the woods with the Doberman barking nonstop behind him. Sweat poured off his face. His heart drummed as he gulped air. What if the pond hadn't separated him from the dog? His knees felt weak. He leaned against a tree to regroup.

"Stay right there, kid."

Badeen stood only ten feet away.

"What's your name, boy?"

"Jason."

"Jason what?" He narrowed the distance between them.

"You know my name."

Badeen grabbed him by the arm and shoved him against a tree.

"You bet I know your name. You're Mike Ferris's kid. Why're you snooping?" He yanked hard on Jason's arm. "Answer me!"

"I hike in the woods all the time."

"You been here before?"

"No."

A look of sadness washed over Badeen's face. "Are you like all the rest? Making me do things I don't want to do? Why do you all do that?"

Jason was too scared to say anything.

"Here I am having a nice day with my momma, poor old lady, and you come along and ruin it. Why'd you do that?"

"I didn't mean to."

The dog kept barking.

"But you did. Now my momma's back there with Rommel breaking her eardrums and upsetting her. I feel so bad and so mad I don't know what to do."

"I'll leave and not come back."

"I have a kid, a good kid. Not a sneaky one who goes around spying on people on their own property. I had a daddy once, too. Not a good daddy. A bad daddy. Mean. Till he disappeared. Nobody else knows what happened to him. I do. He won't hurt nobody no more."

Badeen drew his knife from its sheath on his belt. He pressed the tip of the knife against Jason's throat.

"I should slit your throat and bury you so deep they'd never find you. But my momma's—"

"For walking in the woods?"

"Why was you sneaking away?"

"Nobody messes with a Doberman."

Squinting hard, Badeen drew his head back and spit in Jason's face. "Any ideas about coming back …" With a quick flick of his wrist, he slashed the knife at an angle across Jason's forehead from just over the right eye to the hairline at his left temple. The blade cut to the bone. "… remember this, you sneaky little snot-nose."

Blood streamed into Jason's eyes. The initial stinging sensation of the cut gave way to pain. Jason slapped his hand over the cut. Blood flowed between his fingers and dripped onto the ground. Badeen shoved him hard.

"Don't come back, Ferris! You hear me? Now git!"

Jason, his vision blurred by the blood, ran as fast as he could without ramming into trees. He found his bicycle where he had left it and managed to climb on. Holding the handle bar with one hand while keeping his handkerchief pressed firmly on his forehead with the other, he pedaled back to the Langs'.

Cari and Mrs. Lang stopped the bleeding and applied an antibiotic ointment to the cut. Then they covered the wound with a large gauze patch held in place with white tape.

After supper, Jason begged off when the Langs decided to drive into town to pick up some groceries.

"You'd better lie down so the bleeding doesn't start again," Mrs. Lang said to him. "That's a nasty gash. Barbed wire is nothing to mess with. You're lucky you didn't rip an eye out."

Chapter Twenty-Three

Dusk and thunderheads gathered over the lake as Marvin Pell steered his boat to the landing. As soon as the hull scraped the gravel bottom, Pell swung one fat leg and then the other over the gunwale into the shallow water. From there he pulled the boat far enough onto the landing to back his trailer up and winch the boat onto it.

"That's far enough, Marvin."

Pell twisted around.

Badeen stepped from the shadows, wearing gloves, a pistol in his right hand. "Get back in your boat, Marvin."

"Don't do this, Virgil. Please don't. I ain't said a word to nobody." He backed away from Badeen into deeper water.

Badeen pointed the pistol at the boat. "We need to talk. On the water where no one can listen in."

"I'm beggin' you, Virgil."

Badeen cocked the pistol. Pell, in water up to his crotch, clambered into the stern. Badeen shoved the boat free of the landing, climbed in, and sat at the bow facing Pell.

"Turn on the trolling motor."

"Please, Virgil. I won't ever do nothing to cause trouble. I got a family to take care of. What's done is done."

"The motor."

Pell flipped the toggle switch on the electric motor.

"Take her into the lake. I'll tell you when to stop." He uncocked the pistol.

The trolling motor produced the only sound on the water. The dark lake was calm, its flatness disturbed here and there by an insect or a fish that swirled the water just beneath the surface. Lightning flickered and danced on the western horizon beyond the tree line.

"Far enough."

Pell turned off the motor. "What can I say to change your mind, Virgil?"

"I don't want to do anything, Marvin. I'm only asking you to understand my position. Could you try and do that? No one knows what you know. All I want is to get your attention in case you ever think about yapping."

"You have my attention, had it from the git-go."

"You had to go and have that meeting with Ferris, and now I got someone snooping around my place."

"Who?"

"Ferris's kid. Now ain't that a coincidence?"

"Why, he doesn't know nothing. He wasn't there. Besides, he's just a pup. What could he do?"

"Marvin, I'm a man with responsibilities. My momma's in a wheelchair. I got a son, two dogs. Try to see things from my point of view just for once. Is that asking too much?"

Pell looked as if he wanted to say something but couldn't find the words.

"I'm not going to shoot you. I didn't come here to do that. I'll only do it if you force me to."

"Oh, God, Virgil. Thank you. I thought you was going to kill me." Tears seeped from Pell's eyes and slid down his cheeks.

"Now ease yourself out of the boat and swim for shore. And don't ever forget I could've off'd you right here."

Pell gazed at the distant shore, now lost in shadow and darkness.

"I can't swim that far. I couldn't swim that far even if I had a good heart, which I don't. You know that."

Badeen flicked the pistol for Pell to go over the side.

"You take your choice: water or bullet. The water gives you a chance."

"If they find my body with a bullet hole in it, they'll know I didn't drown. You don't want that. Let's talk this over."

"You think I can't manhandle you off this boat, fat man? Man up and take the chance I'm giving you. If I have to put a bullet in you, I will."

"Damn, Virgil, why—"

"Don't swear! You know I hate it when people swear. There ain't no call for it."

"Look—"

Badeen cocked the pistol.

Pell stared at Badeen, at the water, back at Badeen. In one rocking motion, he pitched off his seat into the water. The splash jogged the boat. Badeen took Pell's place in the stern, started the trolling motor, and steered an oar's length away from Pell, who thrashed and flailed in the dark water. Badeen aimed the pistol at Pell's head.

"Swim!"

"Let me back in the boat! Help me!"

Badeen kept the boat away from Pell, who continued clawing at the water. Pell sank but popped to the surface immediately.

"Help me! Don't let me die like this! You've scared me enough!"

His arms chopped the water until he went under again. He didn't resurface as quickly as before.

"For the love—of God—have mercy on me! Help me, Virgil! Dear—sweet Jesus—oh help me!"

Breathless and gasping, Pell tried to tread water as Badeen eased the boat a few more feet away from him. Pell attempted to stroke toward shore. His effort lasted only a few seconds before it became too strenuous for him. He rolled over on his back and floated while flipping his hands down against the water in a desperate attempt to stay buoyant. Even that proved too much for him.

"Help me, Virgil. Please? You think I'd ever say anything after this? Please, Virgil!"

He began to cry. His feet and legs sank. Vertical, he treaded water again. His sobbing sent spasms through his body that made it more difficult for him to stay afloat. He slipped beneath the surface. Reemerging, he gasped, "My heart! Oh, God!"

He sucked in air with a choking sound. Clutching his

chest, he pitched forward. Nothing but his feet poked out of the water. Then they too disappeared. The water swirled where he struggled beneath the surface. His thrashing ceased. Seconds later, he rose to the surface, his partially submerged body floating face down.

Badeen waited five minutes before heading for shore. At the landing he toggled off the trolling motor and climbed from the boat into the shallow water. He turned the boat around to point it into the lake. Next, he yanked the pull cord of the gas motor. He opened the throttle enough to propel the boat at slow speed. The boat veered off into the darkness of the lake.

Chapter Twenty-Four

Despite the dark clouds that had roiled all day as they trundled eastward, the sky had not surrendered a drop of rain. The August heat had taken its toll weeks earlier on everything green. Now the combination of heat and lack of rain seemed intent on finishing the job.

The Langs' backyard, where Cari and Jason kicked a soccer ball back and forth, was nothing more than a brown expanse broken by forlorn islands of green. Dust that covered the leaves of trees sifted into the air whenever a breeze happened to blow.

"How's your forehead feel?" Cari asked.

Jason ran his hand over the scar. "Still tender but healing okay." They had removed the bandage just yesterday, so the cut remained red and swollen. "I think I'll come to your game tomorrow."

"You've sure been hanging around here a lot lately. How come you're not going to the woods anymore?"

Recalling Badeen's feeding his mother the first spoon of ice cream and how she had beamed with pleasure, Jason shrugged. He also recalled the knife. Two legitimate reasons for him not to go back. He had to leave Badeen behind and get on down his own road.

"Everybody needs a change. I'm not going to the woods anymore."

"You probably shouldn't go off alone like that anyway. That poor Mr. Pell shouldn't have gone fishing alone either."

"What?"

"Didn't you hear? He fell out of his boat and drowned. They found his empty boat, then him. Yesterday."

She kicked the ball. It sailed right past Jason, whose eyes

were riveted on Cari.

"Hello?" Cari said. "Anybody home?"

"Pell was one of the best boatmen around."

"Well, the poor man must have messed up. I'd better get to practice. The new coach has a fit if you're late. Want to go along?"

"I have to check on the puppies and mow the grass. See you later."

"You're going to mow the grass? It's all dead."

"Yeah. Scraggly, isn't it? Mowing will even it out."

She rolled her eyes and smirked.

Black puppies scampered over the garage floor while Jason poured gas into the lawn mower and checked the oil. When he happened to glance up and peer out the window, his breath caught in his throat. A light blue pickup had stopped in front of the Lang house. Cari was talking to the driver.

Jason dashed to the garage door, closed it behind him so the puppies couldn't escape, and darted across the lawn toward Cari, who was still talking to the driver and motioning with her hands. The pickup eased away before Jason reached it.

"What did he want?"

"Directions to the QwikTrip. What a strange-looking man. Polite, though, and nice teeth."

"Did he say anything?"

"He said thanks. Asked me my name and said thanks again. Why are you all worked up?"

Jason's eyes tracked the pickup. A fist extended from the cab. Jason glanced at Cari, then back at the departing truck.

"Don't get bent out of shape, Ferris. A little jealous, maybe?"

Jason continued watching the pickup and said nothing.

Jason had finished mowing the grass and was putting away the lawn mower when a white car turned off the county road and parked on the gravel driveway. Jason recognized the car and the woman who emerged from behind the wheel. He waited for her to approach.

"Hi. Remember me?" she said.

121

"You're Detective Pearson."

"And your name is Jason, right?"

"Yes, ma'am."

"Could we talk a few minutes?"

Jason nodded and headed for the porch. They sat on the steps.

"You heard about Marvin Pell? How they found him in the lake?"

"Yes, ma'am."

"It's pretty common knowledge that four people witnessed what happened to Roger Walker last spring. Now two of them are dead."

She waited for his reaction. Jason gazed at her without replying.

"I know this has been awful for you, Jason. Believe me, I don't want to make it worse. But we have killers on the loose. They've killed before, probably will again. What do you think of that?"

Jason shrugged. Pearson frowned, then smiled.

"I got to thinking after they dragged Mr. Pell from the lake. I thought maybe you might have overheard something. Like, maybe your father talking to your mother, or maybe to Mr. Pell. You ever hear any conversations about what happened to Mr. Walker?"

Jason looked away. Across the road, Mr. Ferguson tended his beehives. Beyond Mr. Ferguson another hundred yards or so a small herd of Holsteins bunched together under a red oak, swishing their tails at flies.

He wanted to tell her everything he knew, but what good would it do? What would come of it? Sure, he had heard what happened. Hadn't seen what happened though. He knew what he knew second-hand. He recalled reading somewhere that lawyers call it hearsay, not worth a hoot in court. And his dad, who had been pretty darn smart, hadn't gone to the police. And why had Badeen stopped to talk to Cari? Everybody knew the whereabouts of the QwikTrip.

"Jason?"

"No, ma'am, I didn't hear a thing."

She stared at him for what seemed like forever before shaking her head and snorting. "Well," she said with a sigh, "I tried."

"If it was murder, I hope you catch who did it."

"I do too, Jason. Believe me, I do. It was murder all right."

"I mean, if I had heard anything, what difference would it make?"

The detective became instantly alert. "Well, just supposing," she said, trying to sound laid back, "not saying you did, but *if* you did, that kind of information would give us enough to haul somebody in."

"Then what?"

"Often times when two or more people commit a crime, one of them will crack and testify against the others to get a lighter sentence. We call it plea bargaining. In a capital case, ratting on the other guy could mean avoiding the death penalty."

"What if they don't?"

"Well, it depends. Things aren't all black and white. Still, third-party testimony helps a lot."

Mr. Ferguson went about his work, as if he lived in another world, a peaceful, innocent world. The cattle beneath the small grove of trees swished their tails to ward off flies.

"A friend at school told me Mr. Badeen has a brother who's really mean too."

"Who's Badeen? I never mentioned any names."

Realizing his slip, Jason remained silent.

"You sure you didn't hear your dad talking about this?"

"Rumors are all over the place."

The detective seemed determined to outwait him. She sat motionless. Jason had to say something.

"There must be some truly evil people in this crazy world."

"We don't hear that word very often anymore. It's a good word for the people we're dealing with. Are you religious, Jason?"

"I think religion is important."

"How important?"

"I want to be a priest someday."

Her eyebrows arched up. "So it would be important to you that evil people be brought to justice to pay for what they did to innocent people, right?"

"Yes, ma'am."

"Did you know the man they killed at the plant was a preacher?"

"I heard that."

"He left a wife and baby."

Jason nodded.

"Don't you think they deserve justice? Isn't that only fair?"

"Yes, ma'am. I wish I could help."

She waited again, apparently hoping he would continue. When he didn't, she extended her hand. "If you remember anything, Jason, call me. Okay?"

"I sure will."

Detective Pearson stood up and slipped a blue leather cardholder from her pocket. "Here's my card. We're here to protect you."

"Thank you, ma'am."

She started for her car.

"A case like this must be a stinking mess. Kind of like boiling cabbage," Jason said.

The detective jerked around. She glared at him and said nothing, but her pursed lips and red face said a lot and so did her heaving chest. After a long moment, she turned on heel and strode to her car. She slammed the door when she got in.

Watching her drive off, Jason marveled at how easily he had lied to her. He didn't really know why he had mentioned the boiling cabbage … or maybe he did.

Why had Badeen talked to Cari?

To satisfy the court, Jason officially lived with the Langs and ate most of his evening meals with them. He otherwise stayed home while Father Ed worked with the authorities to settle his parents' affairs. His father's life insurance had not come through yet.

Jason still wasn't sure how it all worked, but as he understood it, the money would go to the probate court, which would deposit it in the bank because his mother couldn't receive it, and the bank would be custodian of the money.

Meanwhile, Father Ed lent Mr. and Mrs. Lang money for Jason's food, and he paid the mortgage, utilities, and other bills. He also saw to it that Jason had money for food and incidentals, all to be paid back when the insurance companies paid off. Jason didn't know the details, nor did he know where he would go when the authorities settled everything. Father Ed said the house would probably go up for sale before Christmas.

He lay in bed listening to Cari practice the violin. The music she played was one of his favorites, "Ah! Sweet Mystery of Life," a song she had played for the first time on the night Luke died, though he didn't know the title back then. He liked the lyrics of the old song, but the instrumental version, especially when Cari played it on her violin, enthralled him. She had given him the words, which he knew by heart, so whenever she played the song, he recited the words to himself.

The haunting melody always swept away his cares and transformed the night into something sacred. The song also conveyed a definite, though indefinable, sadness.

> *Ah! Sweet mystery of life, at last I've found thee;*
> *Ah! At last I know the secret of it all:*
> *All the longing, seeking, striving, waiting, yearning,*
> *The idle hopes, the joys and burning tears that fall!*
> *For 'tis love, and love alone, the world is seeking;*
> *And it's love, and love alone, I've waited for;*
> *And my heart has heard the answer to its calling*
> *For it is love that rules for evermore!*

Not exactly what St. Paul had in mind when he said, "So there abide faith, hope and charity, these three; but the greatest of these is love." Well, some Bibles, including the Catholic one, said "charity," but most said "love." Either way, the meaning seemed clear enough.

The beauty and mystery of the music symbolized Cari. They conjured up a vision of her that enveloped him in a way that he wished would never end.

What did she have on? Pajamas? Nightgown? T-shirt and panties? Nothing? He took a deep breath and tiptoed to his west window, wondering at the same time why he felt he had to be stealthy about it.

She usually kept her shade drawn but not always. He leaned on the open sill and peered into the cool darkness. So dark. Without moonlight, it even felt dark. No light outlined Cari's window. She often played in the dark. Was she sitting on a chair? Standing? His imagination convinced him that tonight she played her violin naked.

The music stopped. He waited, hoping she would resume playing her music, any music, on this night of all nights, not that he knew why; it was no special night, after all, but he desperately wanted her to play on.

It was not to be. After several minutes, he realized she must have gone to bed, so he got back into bed too, but he couldn't stop thinking about her. He didn't want to do next what he often did when he thought about her. Father Ed always got on his case in the confessional. Yet….

A sound—what was it? Like scrunching on gravel. He slid off the bed and hurried down the hall to the north window. A familiar pickup sat at the end of the drive, still partially on the hard road. The pickup crept ahead and continued west on the asphalt.

Jason grabbed his pants from the hook next to his bed and pulled them on. He bolted down the stairs and out the front door to the edge of the road. The brake lights on the pickup flashed a couple hundred yards away. Feeling with his hands, Jason found a golf ball-size rock.

When the truck executed a U-turn, Jason edged back into the yard and hid behind a large burr oak. The pickup approached slowly until it stopped at the driveway. A minute passed. Then another. The time seemed like an hour. Badeen had to be deaf not to hear the reverberations of Jason's heart or his raspy breathing. Jason could stand it no longer.

"What do you want?" he called out.

"Whoa! You caught me off guard. Past your bedtime, ain't it? I'm keeping tabs on you, boy. Want to make sure you're all right. You doin' okay? I mean, okay for an orphan?"

"I'm doing great."

Badeen giggled. "Ain't you a little scared? I would be. Come on, you might as well admit it."

"What if I am? So what?"

Badeen giggled again.

"I hear your old lady took a one-way drive to the funny farm. That makes me sad. I'd hate to see my momma go to the funny farm. Does it make you sad?"

Jason didn't reply.

"What's the matter, cat got your tongue? Bet you really like your blonde girlie friend next door. She's a looker. Such a nice shape and blue eyes. Be too bad if something happened to her."

"Let her alone! She has nothing to do with this!"

"Oh yes she does."

Jason stepped out from behind the tree. "You are evil! Why does God let you live?" He threw the rock as hard as he could. It cracked into the side of the pickup.

The silence that followed for several moments nearly sent Jason running to the house. Then Badeen's disembodied voice penetrated the darkness. "Why did you do that? My little boy wouldn't do that. He's just a pup, but he has good manners. You are definitely making me think bad thoughts. Very bad thoughts. I really hate it when people do that."

"Why don't you let us alone?"

"It ain't that simple, boy."

"She doesn't know a thing about you or what happened."

"Now, how can I be sure of that?"

"I give you my word."

"You know what? I'd like to take your word on it. Don't think I can, though. If you was like my boy, I would. I'm afraid you're like all the rest."

"Damn you! You're a monster. I hope you burn in hell forever!"

"Now there ain't no call to talk like that. I mean, that is plain *mean*. And I hate your bad language. Why do you talk like that? I never use swear words. It ain't polite."

Dead silence pervaded the night.

"You'd rather kill people."

No sound came from the truck. What would Badeen do? The words must have stung him. Although the air wasn't cold, Jason's entire body shook. He wished he hadn't said what he had.

"I could take you out right now or anytime, but I'm not going to," Badeen said. "No, I won't never lay a hand on you. Not never. I want you to live a long time, so's you can think about everything that happened this summer.

"Your doggie—such a nice friendly doggie—ran into a little trouble. Then your weak-kneed daddy dangled hisself at the end of a rope. Such a terrible waste of good rope. You hauled your momma to the loony bin. And poor Marvin Pell took a swim. Ain't you going to have fond memories? Let's see, what else could happen?"

"Stay away from Cari, or I'll kill you!"

Badeen giggled. "Now that's a good one, sweetie-pie. I like a good sense of humor." He stopped speaking for what seemed forever. Then, "Tell your girlie friend to be real careful."

The headlights flashed on. The truck hurtled eastward through the blackness until its taillights faded.

He likes to hurt people, Mr. Ferris.

Distant church bells tolled midnight.

128

PART II

Chapter Twenty-Five

2007

Saint Victor Hall, a renovated nineteenth century relic on the campus of Saint Victor College, retained a certain bookish mustiness about it in spite of its remodeled brightness. Some, though not all, found the dichotomy satisfying.

The old building had survived for well over one hundred years and remained strong enough to withstand structural changes needed to accommodate the demands of new technology and new generations of students and faculty. Many chose to see it as a symbol of twenty-first century renewal within the ancient traditions of the Catholic Church. Others saw an old building that needed razing.

Today in classroom 422 two front row students, a male and female, spoke with passion to each other at the same time. Other students raised their hands. Some of them shouted over the two front row students. Intensity permeated the room.

"How can you say that?" a student cried out from the back of the room. "It's insane. Immoral!"

"*You're* insane! Two wrongs don't make a right!"

"She's right!"

"No, she's not!"

"There's another approach!"

"Father, I want the floor!"

His right index finger caressing the brass violin medallion on the left lapel of his black suit, Father Jason Ferris listened intently amid the tumult. He formed a T with his hands. The students stopped talking.

"Thank you for that spirited debate. You nailed it."

"Which side are you on, Father?"

"Both," he said with a smile.

"How can that be?"

"Think about it."

"We never have enough time," another student said. "You can't figure these things out in a class period."

Jason smiled. "Then keep thinking when you leave. The proposition for next time: We don't do as we *believe*. We actually end up believing as we *do*. Please be fully prepared to defend or attack, including concrete examples."

"Could you repeat that, Father?"

He did and the students wrote down the assignment.

"Could you give us more to go on, Father?"

"No. Just think about it. Okay, let's clear out."

Another instructor and students clamored at the door for the next class period, but no one in the room showed any inclination to leave.

"Don't forget your bugle tomorrow night, Father. We've got to beat the Bees!"

The other students supported the request by acclamation. Jason flashed thumbs up. The students rose but didn't leave.

"Father, we're sorry about your mother," one said.

"Thank you. She died peacefully."

The students bustled to the exit. One student, Dan Petrakis, a varsity basketball player, approached the front of the room.

"Father, could I see you?"

"Sure. Right now okay?"

"It's kind of personal. Might take more than a few minutes, you know?"

Jason took a daily planner from his coat pocket and opened it. "I'm jammed today. Can you come to my room tonight at nine-thirty? I should be out of my last committee meeting by then."

"Sure thing, Father. Beckman Hall, right?"

Jason nodded, greeted the incoming instructor, and headed for the door. Students crowded into the room and took their seats for the next class.

"Got your bugle ready for the game, Father?" one asked.

Jason winked and raised his right fist. Several students took this as their cue to get into cheering mode.

"All right!"

"Be ready to rumble!"

"Beat the Bees!"

Chapter Twenty-Six

Jason glanced at his watch. It was nearly nine-thirty. He had just returned to his apartment in Beckman Hall and expected Dan Petrakis momentarily. He repaired to his kitchenette, quickly mixed a pitcher of lime Kool-Aid, poured himself a glass with ice, and set it on his desk in his living room next to a picture of Cari. A life-size wood crucifix stood in the center of the small room, with an old dented bugle hanging from the nail in Christ's right hand.

A knock on the door.

"Come in."

Dan entered looking nervous. Jason took his coat and hung it on a hook next to the door.

"Have a chair. Kool-Aid?"

"No, thanks, Father."

Jason sat across from the young man. "Okay, what's up?"

"Well, ah, it's like this …."

"Girl trouble?"

Dan's head jerked. "Well, yeah."

"Girl *in* trouble?"

Clearly uncomfortable, Dan nodded.

"Do you love her?"

The student nodded vigorously. "Sure do, Father. I want to marry her."

"Do it. Don't hesitate. Work for a semester if you must."

"My parents will go ballistic. They like her enough, but this isn't part of the game plan."

"Which is?"

"Get my degree, go for the MBA, and join the family business."

"What's their objection? Her religion? Race? Flat feet?"

Dan laughed. "She's beautiful and smart, Father, and has the greatest personality in the world."

"I feel a 'however' coming up."

"She's Jewish, Father."

Jason took a sip of Kool-Aid. "A different religion can be right up there with race when it comes to potential conflict."

"I know. I don't think it'll be a problem with us. I mean, we're on the same page with everything."

"That page being?"

"Well, we think the same. About money, politics, the number of kids we want. Right down the line, you know?"

"I take it she has no desire to convert."

Dan combed his fingers through his hair. "We haven't really discussed it. But no, she doesn't want to change."

"You need to bring it out into the open. She either will or won't. May I assume you wish to remain Catholic?"

"Beyond a doubt, Father. No way am I changing."

"Her feelings are equally legitimate and may be equally as strong. You have to respect that. Could be confusing to the kids and a real bone of contention between the two of you."

"Yeah, guess so."

"Unless you address it right now and stick with whatever you decide."

Dan waited for him to continue.

"Okay, here's the deal. You're over twenty-one. Your responsibilities supersede your parents' at this point, though you must continue to honor them and give their wishes consideration.

"Your immediate choices are two: get married or give the child up for adoption. And then take a good hard look at your options. Tough decisions are painful, but if we avoid or postpone them, we pay a heavy attritional price. With me so far?"

"I think so."

"You may not come to agreement. For example, you may agree not to marry and she might decide to keep the child. You'd be financially responsible for eighteen years. Also, are her parents well off, or would she face financial hardship?"

"Her parents have dough. Why?"

"Because otherwise she'd be at a real disadvantage in your discussions. She'd be even more fearful and vulnerable than she would be otherwise and might agree to things because of her fears, even if in her heart she felt it was wrong. Later, her true feelings would surface, probably laced with resentment and—boom! Problems galore.

"I won't presume to tell you what to do. Be a good son. Discuss the situation with your parents. Try to arrive at a decision everyone can live with. If you decide to marry, commit yourself to her and love her as if your life depended on it. Because it does."

Dan fiddled with a button on his shirt.

"Another thing. What if she wants to get an abortion?"

"No way! That's my kid, too!"

"Could be on the table. Women hold the power in that scenario. You'd better think it through. There could be one further scenario. She could deliver the baby and let you raise it. Highly unlikely, but possible. What are your feelings about that?"

"Jeez, Father, I never thought about it."

"You'd carry a lot of responsibility. And whenever you dated, you'd have a kid in your picture. Actually, the child will be part of your résumé whether it's in your care or hers. It's normally the other way around, with the woman having a child or two in tow, but what if you had to do the raising?"

He waited for the student to react.

Dan rubbed the stubble on his chin. "The whole deal is really complicated."

"Daylight illuminates better than moonlight, my friend. Let me paraphrase a passage from somewhere, maybe Shakespeare: 'Too soon the plaintive call of the nightingale gives way to the ribald cackling of the crows.' You don't have to eat crow, but you'd better be able to talk crow."

"Man, that's the truth. I don't want to take any more of your time, Father. Sounds like you've had a long day."

"We can talk as long as you want. Or we can talk another day. Your call."

"I need to do some heavy thinking." He arose to leave. "Thanks a lot, Father."

"Don't mention it. In the meantime, score twenty against St. Ambrose tomorrow night."

"The Bees are tough."

"Less than twenty and you are excommunicated from basketball."

Dan laughed, then turned serious.

"Will you hear my confession, Father?"

Jason swung off the chair and poured another glass of Kool-Aid. He motioned to Dan with the pitcher. The student shook his head.

"I'm probably one of the few people who still drinks this stuff, but I love it. Bet I drink more than anybody else on the planet. Let's pass for now on the confession. Momentary remorse over sex gets me right here." He jabbed his fist into his stomach with a dramatic grimace. Noticing Dan's puzzled reaction, he waved his hand and smiled. "Be honest. You're not sorry for the sex. You regret the consequences, not the sex itself. True or false?"

"Yeah, you're right."

Jason drank his Kool-Aid and swirled the ice cubes. He reached over and cuffed Dan on the shoulder. "Intercourse with the woman you love wasn't a mortal blow to your soul. It's what you do from now on that counts. With your woman, with your child. Love them and protect them, whatever you end up deciding. By all means, protect them." He motioned to the door. "Come on. You need a good night's sleep."

They shook hands at the door. Jason threw his arm over Dan's shoulders. The telephone rang behind them.

"You're a good man, Daniel Petrakis. Come and see me any time."

"Thanks, Father. Sorry about your mother. Your dad doing okay?"

The phone rang again.

"He died when I was fourteen."

"Bummer. Well, I'd better hit the sack."

Jason closed the door and hurried to the ringing phone.

"Father Ferris here." He listened for a moment. "Yes, Monsignor. I'll come right over." He hung up the phone and glanced at the clock. Why would the monsignor summon him so late?

After throwing on his coat and a Russian fur hat, he touched the bugle on the crucifix before leaving to see his mentor Monsignor Korth, whom Jason would succeed as spiritual director of the college, a post he wanted more than any other in the college community.

He leaned into a biting west wind and hunched his way up the sloping hill and across the Commons to the most imposing building on campus: Duquesne Hall, the original dormitory connected to Christ the King chapel by an ambulatory.

The bitter cold had chilled him to the bone by the time he entered the building and took the elevator to Monsignor Korth's apartment on the north wing of the fourth floor. The monsignor had told him the door would be unlocked and to come in.

Jason found the monsignor lying in a bed straddled by a hospital table covered with numerous items—water, baby aspirin, metoprolol, a vial of nitroglycerine, facial tissue, two books and a *Time* magazine.

"Good evening, Monsignor."

"Thank you for coming, Jason. Here, move this table away."

Korth was eighty-five but alert in spite of his illness. Jason rolled the table to the foot of the bed.

"Welcome back. My condolences. Your mother could not have been old."

"Fifty-eight."

The old man shook his head. "My mother died at eighty-four. Worst time of my life. You're in for a tough year ahead." Korth turned his head and coughed several times. Reaching for a tissue, he blew his nose and dropped the white tissue into a wastebasket at the side of the bed. "A head cold on top of everything else. The retreat plans progress?"

"We're muddling along."

Korth chuckled. "The same story every year. I organized the annual retreat for forty-five years, and it always spiraled down to the last minute. Please take off your coat and have a chair."

Jason did so and waited for the monsignor, who was not one for small talk, to continue.

"You don't parade your piety. On the contrary, you mask it. One more speeding ticket and you can probably say goodbye to your license forever. God only knows how many times the police have let you off with a warning.

"You drink beer with students, blow on that damn bugle of yours at the drop of a miter, and they respond like lemmings." He laughed softly. "Refreshing, in my estimation. Beneath all of that, in your heart of hearts, you are isolated from students and faculty alike. From me."

Clearing his throat, he motioned for water, which Jason poured for him and waited while he drank it.

"Thank you. Where was I? Oh yes. You stir the water as routinely as you shave. You advocate the ordination of women. You challenge clerical celibacy. You question the Church's stance on birth control. You shout from the rooftops that we are punished not so much *for* our sins as *by* our sins.

"And yet in many ways you are a traditionalist, a throwback to my time. You despise guitar masses in favor of pipe organs. You love the Gregorian chant; you're the best chanter we have. If you had your way, every mass would be a high mass that would take two hours from start to finish."

Korth looked closely at Jason. "I bore you with stale news. When did you decide to become a priest?"

"I've always wanted to be a priest."

"Why?"

Jason shifted in his chair and stroked the diagonal scar on his forehead.

"Do we ever really know, Monsignor?"

Korth gestured impatiently with his hands. "Take a stab at it. Certainly you had reasons. Articulate them for me. Might help us both. And some day you might call me Joe, like everybody else around here." The smile and the twinkle in his eye were genuine.

Jason had liked the man since their first meeting. His admiration and respect for his mentor had deepened over the years. At this moment, however, a wave of unease swept over him. Korth had a PhD in psychology and his powers of perception were legendary at Saint Victor. Although typically quite direct, his directness often disguised a subtext that became apparent only in retrospect, if at all. Jason had the distinct feeling that Korth's directness tonight was pure and that he would drive to a point quickly.

"My mother called me her miracle baby. The doctors had told her she could never conceive. At my birth, she saw me as a gift from God. I wanted to be a priest by my first communion."

"Nothing out of the ordinary there. Is there more? Since my ordination sixty years ago, believe me, I've seen my share of phonies in Roman collars. You are the genuine article. Unorthodox and theologically feisty, but genuine. That's one of the reasons you will succeed me as spiritual director of the college. Everyone knows and welcomes that, but something is missing.

"Be that as it may, I believe you carry a heavy secret, one that is incompatible with your vocation. The signs have become more pronounced of late."

"I've no idea—"

"My instincts in these matters are seldom off the mark. Share your burden with a dying friend. Is it a woman? Perhaps the one whose picture adorns your desk?"

Jason gazed at the old priest for a long moment.

"Do you have any Scotch, Monsignor?"

Korth laughed. "Not quite the response I expected, but an excellent one." He pointed. "There, first shelf of the hutch. I'll join you. By the way, do you sleep in that collar? I expected to see you in more casual dress at this hour."

Jason smiled as he retrieved the Scotch. Pausing, he said, "Should you...I mean, your heart...."

"Do you think I still worry about my health? Or do you think St. Peter might object to whisky on my breath? Ha! I hope he has an infinite supply up there."

Jason extracted a bottle of Dewar's and two glasses. His hand shook when he poured the liquor.

"There's ice in the fridge. I'll take mine neat, no ice, thanks."

Jason handed Korth his drink and opened the small black refrigerator next to the hutch.

"Yes, Monsignor, there is a woman. I love her more than anything else in the world." He swirled the ice in his glass. The subdued light endowed the Scotch with a rich golden glow.

"Your pause is six months pregnant."

"It's late. Perhaps another time...."

"Don't even think about leaving on that note."

Jason sipped his Scotch, not at all certain he wanted to continue. His collar chafed the side of his neck, as it always did. He decided to plunge ahead.

"It's a long story that involves so much more than the woman. I'll share it with you in confidence but not as a confession." He took a sip of his whisky. "In fact, I'll share it in minute detail—more detail than you want—so that you might experience to some degree what I did and feel what I felt. Even so, I don't expect you to perceive my experience as I did.

"One further condition, Monsignor: You must hear me out without interruption. I'll attempt to remember and convey every word, many of which are so imbedded in my memory that I could never forget them. I will find the narrative difficult at times, but I don't want a dialogue. Do you accept?"

"What other choice do I have?"

Jason tipped his glass for a good swallow of Scotch. "When I was fourteen, my father was forced to watch a murder at the plant where he worked. Two men threw a third man into a pulp vat, a completely premeditated killing. One of the perpetrators had killed before. They warned my father and the other witness not to say a word, or they would kill them and their families. My father couldn't cope with the pressure. Our happy family began to unravel."

Jason related the changes in his father's personality and behavior, and narrated events up to the time Badeen parked in front of the Ferris home late at night....

1986

"I hear your old lady took a one-way drive to the funny farm. That makes me sad. I'd hate to see my momma go to the funny farm. Does it make you sad?"

I didn't reply.

"What's the matter, cat got your tongue? Bet you really like your blonde girlie friend next door. She's a looker. Such a nice shape and blue eyes. Be too bad if something happened to her."

"Let her alone! She has nothing to do with this!"

"Oh yes she does."

I stepped out from behind the tree and screamed, "You are evil! Why does God let you live?" and threw the rock as hard as I could. The rock cracked into the side of the pickup. I almost lost my nerve in the silence that followed. I wanted to run far, far away. Then Badeen's voice broke the stillness.

"Now why did you do that? My little boy wouldn't do that. He's just a pup, but he has good manners. You are definitely making me think bad thoughts. Very bad thoughts. I hate it when people do that."

"Why don't you let us alone?"

"It ain't that simple, boy."

"She doesn't know a thing about you or what happened."

"Now, how can I be sure of that?"

"I give you my word."

"You know what? I'd like to take your word on it. Don't think I can, though. Nope, I sure can't. If you was like my boy, I would. You're like all the rest. And I got my momma to worry about."

"Damn you! You're a monster. I hope you burn in hell forever!"

"Now, there ain't no call to talk like that. I mean, that is plain *mean*. And I hate your bad language. Shame on you. Why do you talk like that? I never use swear words. It ain't polite."

"You'd rather kill people."

Not a sound from inside the truck. What would Badeen do? My words must have stung him. The air wasn't cold, but my entire body shook. I wished I hadn't said what I had.

"I could take you out right now or anytime, but I'm not going to," Badeen said. "No, I won't ever lay a hand on you. Not never. I want you to live a long time, so you can think about everything that happened this summer.

"Your doggie—such a friendly little doggie—ran into some trouble. Then your weak-kneed daddy dangled hisself at the end of a rope. Terrible waste of good rope, I say. You hauled your momma to the loony bin. And poor Marvin Pell took a swim. Ain't you going to have fond memories? Let's see, what else could happen?"

"Stay away from Cari or I'll kill you!"

Badeen giggled. "Now, that's a good one, sweetie-pie. I like a good sense of humor. Tell your girlie friend to be real careful."

The headlights flashed on. The truck hurtled eastward through the darkness until its taillights faded into the night.

I recalled the detective's words as distant church bells tolled the midnight hour: *He likes to hurt people, Mr. Ferris.*

Chapter Twenty-Seven

Needless to say, I didn't get any sleep for the rest of that night. I was scared out of my wits but resolute and had a lot of thinking to do.

The next morning, Saturday, I biked over to the library on Exchange Street, not far from the Unified Dairy, and proceeded directly to the reference desk.

It didn't take me long to find the information. I selected three books, carried them to a table, and began reading and taking notes. Then I found material on another matter. A crucial matter. So crucial that my life depended on it.

My research completed, I rode my bike over to the Unified Dairy and asked to see the owner, Mr. Elber, a good guy liked by everybody.

"Hi, Jason. How's the world treating you?"

"Just fine, sir. I need to ask a favor."

"Fire away."

"I want to get an early start on a school project, and I need a little banana oil. Do you have any?"

"Sure do. How much do you need?"

"Just a few ounces."

"Hang on." He disappeared. When he returned, he handed me a small plastic jar of liquid.

"Here you go," he said.

"How much do I owe you?"

"Don't embarrass me, son," he said with a smile.

"Thank you, Mr. Elber."

"You're welcome. I'm really sorry about your folks, Jason. You doing okay?"

I nodded and thanked him for asking. Then I biked home.

That night I laid several items on the concrete floor of the garage: a chisel, a flashlight, a five-foot section of two-by-four board, a nylon backpack, a pair of white gloves, a canister of Yard Guard wasp repellant, an old pair of tennis shoes, a washrag, five tubes of liquid weld, and some bungee cords.

After a moment of thought, I replaced the liquid weld on a shelf. I wouldn't need it until I had successfully completed other parts of my plan. If unsuccessful I wouldn't need it or anything else.

I filled a one-quart plastic oil container with gasoline from the lawn mower gas can and screwed on the lid. Next, I shoved the washrag and a box of wooden matches into my pocket, picked up the flashlight, went to the garage door, and turned off the overhead light.

I crossed the road, climbed over a fence, and strode through the August weeds along a gently sloping knoll. Moonlight and my familiarity with the terrain rendered the flashlight unnecessary.

I went to Clem Ferguson's beehives where I selected one about the size of a medium Styrofoam cooler and plugged the entrance with the washrag. Picking up the hive—floor, brood chamber, and roof—I carried all of it back to our garage.

With everything set to go and nothing more to do until morning, I climbed into bed. The sound of Cari's violin floated through the night with the bittersweet notes of "Somewhere, My Love," one of my favorite songs then and my hands-down, all-time favorite now. When she stopped playing, I slept soundly in spite of my raging anxiety.

Chapter Twenty-Eight

On Sunday morning I woke up early. Cari, her parents, and I ate breakfast together, one of the few times I had joined them for anything other than evening meal.

To defray the cost of my food, the custodian of my dad's insurance money had begun paying them a hundred dollars a month, which to me seemed insufficient to cover three meals a day. Besides that, I preferred eating alone most of the time. I had become a loner in many ways.

"What're you doing today, Jason?" Mrs. Lang asked.

"I think I'll bike over to Hogback and hike along Richland Creek before I go to mass."

"Thought you were tired of the woods," Cari said. A deaf person would have detected the recrimination in her voice.

"One last time."

"Oh, I suppose for old times' sake? You and the rest of the squirrels?"

"Guess you could say that."

"I'll go with you."

"Aren't you going to practice?"

"That stupid coach can yell at someone else. Practice on Sunday. The coach is a creep! I should go to church. I'd be excused if I did."

"You could tell him you go to church."

"Oh sure. Just lie about it, huh? Some priest you'll be."

"Now, Cari," Mrs. Lang said.

I took a bite of toast. She could not come with me at any cost. "Where I'm going has really thick undergrowth. Full of snakes, too."

"You lie like a rug, Ferris. And you don't scare me for a second."

Mrs. Lang said, "Maybe Jason wants to be alone."

"So tell me something new. Fine. Go take your stupid hike. I don't want to go anyway."

Cari threw her napkin on the table and tromped out of the kitchen. Her mother watched her with apprehension.

"Seems she's up and down like a yo-yo these days. Must be the weather," Mr. Lang said.

Mrs. Lang shot him a certain you-are-an-idiot look that women hold in reserve for their husbands. Thank goodness, the doorbell rang just as I pushed my chair back from the table.

"I'll get it," I said.

At the front door, I found myself face-to-face with Sinkhorn. My heart jackhammered.

"You the folks with the free pups?"

I couldn't find my tongue.

"The black Labs," Sinkhorn said.

"They're all gone."

"Already? The ad just ran today."

"We've had a sign up." I pointed to a sign in the yard. "One man took three."

Sinkhorn studied me. I had the feeling he could read my thoughts. Or at least sense my lies.

"Don't I know you? I've seen you somewhere."

"No, sir. I don't think so."

"How many were there?"

"Eight." One more than the actual litter.

"Could I see the bitch?"

"She got run over by a car."

Sinkhorn's eyes narrowed.

"Eight, huh?" He turned to leave but whirled around. "You sure we don't know each other?"

"Yes, sir."

As he strutted to his motorcycle, his body language told me he was reluctant to leave before he had placed me. He leaned against his machine and scanned the Lang home—the lawn, the house, the garage—as if trying to connect some elusive dots, head cocked up at the sky, countenance furrowed.

He finally threw his leg over his motorcycle and roared off. I can't begin to describe my feeling of dread. I nearly decided to cancel my plans.

The Green Bay Packer T-shirt I always wore when I spied on Badeen and Sinkhorn smelled and needed washing, a condition that wouldn't matter much in a few hours. I had all my supplies laid out neatly on the workbench next to the beehive and my backpack. I stuffed my father's loaded nine-millimeter pistol into the backpack.

I almost jumped off the floor when Cari barged in wearing her soccer uniform. She laughed at my jumpiness.

"Little goosey today? What are you doing?"

"Nothing."

"I can see you're doing *something*. Why are you being so sneaky and dorky? I mean, more than usual."

"Aren't you late for soccer?"

"What's in the box? What's that buzzing sound?"

She reached out to touch the hive I had taken from Mr. Ferguson.

"Don't!"

She drew her hand back as if she had touched a hot stove. With a sidelong glance at me, she tapped the hive. The buzzing increased.

"Jeez Louise, Ferris. Is that full of bees, or what?"

"Sure it is. It's a beehive. I'm going to turn them loose."

"Then why have them in the box in the first place?"

"Cari!" Mrs. Lang called from next door. "Time to go."

"Ferris, you are getting totally weird."

She slapped the hive. The buzzing got louder.

Chapter Twenty-Nine

Wearing a dark gray jacket, gloves, shorts and old sneakers, I knelt in a stand of jack pine behind Badeen's outhouse, which stood not far from his house and directly opposite my usual hiding place when I spied on him.

The section of board, the beehive, and the backpack lay beside me on the ground. The canister of Yard Guard protruded from my right jacket pocket.

I knew that Badeen arose later on Sunday but not this late, not past eight. Sinkhorn would arrive by eight-thirty. I had to deal with Badeen before Sinkhorn showed up. A foreboding of disaster washed over me, followed by doubt. Not only my hands, but my entire body shook uncontrollably. Sweat rolled off my face. I could hardly breathe. Mosquitos swarmed over me.

Badeen should have been up by now for his morning trip to the outhouse. Where could he be? What was he doing?

I saw movement at the corner of Badeen's house. Pistol on hip, Badeen sauntered up the path to the outhouse. Why on this day of all days did he walk in such slow motion? He stopped midway to stretch and run his hands through his hair.

Badeen's white lapdog trailed behind him. My heart sank. Never before had Badeen brought the dog with him on his morning trip to the outhouse. Everything was going wrong.

Was that the distant sound of a motorcycle? I listened carefully, but didn't hear the distinct, guttural roar of a Harley. I glanced at my watch. It was eight-sixteen.

Badeen disappeared from view when he reached the outhouse. I heard him open the door and scuffle in. As usual, he didn't close the door.

I shoved the chisel between the outer roof and the wall of

the hive. The tip of the chisel punctured the propolis—a glue bees make to seal their hives—and quickly pried the roof loose, but kept it in place to keep the bees from escaping.

Next, I extracted the jar of banana oil from my pocket, unscrewed the cap, and dribbled the liquid liberally on the top and sides of the hive. Then I shook the hive hard. The bees inside immediately began buzzing loudly. I returned the empty jar to my pocket.

The lapdog rounded the outhouse. She must have picked up my scent or that of the banana oil. She began yapping as only a frightened small dog can.

"Tootsie!" Badeen grunted. "Quiet!"

Tootsie didn't stop. She barked and clawed the ground in a frenzy. I had to act fast.

"Tootsie!" Badeen shouted. "Knock it off!"

I picked up the board and hive and hurried to the side of the outhouse. Dropping the board, I gripped the hive by the floor and brood chamber with both hands.

"Who's that? What—"

I rounded the corner of the outhouse into Badeen's line of sight as he sat on the toilet. I hurled the hive at him. The roof of the hive tumbled off as Badeen reflexively caught the hive in his arms. A swarm of bees exploded into his face.

"Wha—You son of a bitch! Aaaaaieeeeee!"

The lapdog scampered off.

I slammed the door shut, jammed the two-by-four into the dirt, and wedged it against the door. Badeen screamed and thrashed inside. The outhouse tipped and shook so badly I thought it would topple over. Incoherent shrieking fractured the Sunday morning silence.

The Doberman streaked up the path. I pulled the wasp repellant from my pocket. The outhouse door broke down under Badeen's weight and tremendous strength. He lunged out and lurched down the path screaming and slapping at the bees with one hand while trying to hold his pants up with the other. His screams stopped abruptly when he had gone only a short distance.

I aimed the repellant at the charging Doberman. A fog

enveloped the dog. He kept coming. Finally, only a yard or two from me, the dog yelped and began scraping his face along the ground and rubbing his eyes with his paws. I kept spraying into the dog's face until he retreated in pain after his master. I grabbed the backpack and followed.

Badeen had jumped into the pond to escape the bees that now flew in a frenzy above the water. Every time Badeen broke the surface, the bees forced him under again. Oddly, he never screamed or made any other sound.

The Doberman, snorting and whining and rubbing his face, kept his distance from me. Badeen floated to the surface for the last time, face down. I yanked off my gloves.

That's when my plan began to fall apart.

A motorcycle downshifted on the gravel driveway behind me. I wheeled around and grabbed the backpack. I fumbled with it in a vain attempt to get my father's pistol.

Sinkhorn rolled up to me on his Harley. He braked hard and skidded to a stop.

"What the hell?" Sinkhorn leaped off the cycle. "You again!" Then he saw Badeen's body in the pond. "You little bastard!"

Sinkhorn rushed at me, an expression of pure hate on his face. I spun around and jumped into the pond feet first. Nearly chest deep in water, I thrashed away from shore and dove towards Badeen. Sinkhorn splashed into the water behind me.

Sinkhorn's fingers scraped my feet. I twisted to get face-up under Badeen's feet as Sinkhorn clawed at me. I kicked furiously to keep him from getting a good hold. Badeen's body rolled, his pants bunched around his ankles. I frantically groped at them.

Just as Sinkhorn's hands tightened on my foot, I felt the grip of Badeen's pistol. Sinkhorn worked his way up my body and clutched my throat. I jammed the pistol into his ribs.

The pistol sounded like a bomb when it fired. Pain exploded in my ears.

Sinkhorn's grip went slack. We both broke the surface gasping. Sinkhorn gasped for much more than momentary breath. He stared at me with a look I'll never forget.

I raised the pistol out of the water. When I aimed it at Sinkhorn's forehead, I saw another expression I'll never forget—the recognition of imminent death and ultimate despair. I hesitated. In that split second of hesitation, hatred and maybe hope returned to his eyes.

I squeezed the trigger. The bullet entered his forehead, obliterated the back of his skull, and sprayed his brains on the water and vegetation at pond's edge. The force of the bullet slammed him backward. He sloshed beneath the surface.

His blood billowed in the water toward me. I tried to circle around the blood, not wanting it to touch me. Of course, it already had and would remain on me forever.

The Doberman showed no inclination to come near me when I scrambled up the bank. Picking up my gloves from the ground, I tugged them on and wiped the pistol thoroughly. I reentered the pond, waded out to Badeen's body, and slid the gun back into its holster.

A near disaster had turned into an incredibly good piece of luck. My plan had been to shoot Badeen if the bee attack failed. After that, I would have lain in wait for Sinkhorn and shot him point-blank. Then, after forcing liquid weld down the barrel to preclude ballistics testing, I would have encased the pistol in liquid weld before enclosing it in cement and dropping it into a lake as far away as I could reasonably convey it on my bike. Using Badeen's gun made all of that unnecessary.

I returned to the outhouse to retrieve the two-by-four and hive. My legs turned rubbery when I looked inside. Chunks of honeycomb and blobs of honey littered the floor and stool. The hive lay in pieces. I began picking up the honey and comb. When I tried to throw them into the undergrowth behind the outhouse, they stuck to my gloves.

Stripping off the wet, sticky gloves proved clumsy, but I managed to get them off and lay them on the backpack. I scraped up all the honey and comb I could with my bare hands. Of course, I couldn't get it all. I did, however, gather up the entire hive.

I collected all my stuff. About halfway to Sinkhorn's

place by way of the woods, I came to the stream that ran along his property. I took off the gloves and laid them in the weeds. On the upended hive, I draped the washrag, wet sneakers, and gloves, then poured the gasoline over the entire heap and placed the empty container on top. One wood match from the backpack, tossed from five feet away, set the pile ablaze.

While the fire burned, I stabbed the board into the mud beneath the shallow water of the stream and pressed the entire length of it well into the mud. I found a heavy rock and shoved it into the mud over the board. If some day the two-by-four floated free, it would pose no threat to me.

I rinsed off my hands in the creek. The hive, constructed of old weathered wood, burned readily. I ground the ashes into the earth. As an added precaution, I reentered the creek and, cupping my hands, splashed water on the ashes until they seeped, practically invisible, into the weeds. I pitched the few remaining chunks of charred board into the stream. There would be no trace of any of it in a matter of days.

I stripped down and dressed in dry clothes from the backpack. I stuffed all the wet things, including the jacket, into the backpack. After surveying the area one last time, I slipped my arms through the backpack straps and hurried to my bike. The bungee cords I had used to transport the hive were still stretched securely around the frame.

My ears still rang from the underwater gunshot.

Chapter Thirty

I rode my bike into the Lang yard where Cari lay on a blanket in a revealing two-piece bathing suit, reading a magazine. She rolled onto her back and braced herself on her elbows when I coasted up to her, a more welcome sight than I could have hoped for, the antidote for all the poison in my once healthy world.

"Did you have fun all by your lonesome?" Her words dripped sarcasm.

"Mission accomplished. What are you reading?"

"Just an old *Cosmopolitan*. Why'd you change your clothes? You had on a jacket and a Packer shirt earlier. And shorts."

Her remark jump-started my pulse rate. My head dropped down to my plain white T-shirt and jeans. How could I have been so careless? I locked my eyes onto hers.

"I fell into the creek by Kuhlemeyer's foot bridge. Really felt dumb, you know?"

"You had dry clothes with you? Even shoes? You *are* weird."

"Well, I, you know…."

Cari's expression revealed skepticism and amusement. The lump in my throat felt like a baseball. Cari never missed a thing. Why, after all my planning, had I been so stupid as to go anywhere near her before I had gone home and thought through the last details?

She smirked. "Caught you, didn't I?" she teased. Her expression revealed her racing mind. Water dripped from the backpack and ran into my pants.

"You're probably meeting some slut in the woods. J. Ferris: kinky priest."

I laughed, trying to cover my nervousness. If she sensed how nervous I was, she would grill me until I screwed up. "I need a kinky shower," I said, thankful that her hormones outpaced her curiosity.

She stretched her arms over her head and fell back on the blanket. The swimsuit bottom pulled tight against her crotch to leave very little to my imagination.

She abruptly sat up, wrapped her legs under herself Indian-fashion, and leaned forward, her breasts nearly spilling from her top.

"You're hiding something, Jason. What is it?"

"None of your nosey business," I said jokingly.

"You may as well tell me. You know I'll find out."

"No you won't. See you later. After I shower."

"The way your backpack is dripping, you *are* a shower. Get rid of your bees?"

"Yep. They're heroes and free as the wind."

"Do seminaries actually let geeks like you in? Sure glad I'm a Methodist."

Mrs. Lang called out to me. I found her snapping green beans when I entered the kitchen door.

"Can you serve ten-thirty mass?" she asked. "Larry McGraw is going down to a Cubs game and needs a sub. He's already called Father Ed."

"Sure. Thanks."

"Oh, someone called about the pups. I told her we had one left, so she's coming over at six. She wants the mother, too."

"Great!"

I dumped all my wet things into our basement stationary tub and returned my father's pistol, unfired, to where he had always kept it. In the shower I scrubbed myself until the hot water ran out, my hands rubbed nearly raw by the time I finished. When I slid the shower curtain back, Cari stood a few feet away. Shocked, I neither spoke nor covered myself.

"Thought you might stay in there till you melted and ran down the drain," she said.

Her gaze dropped down my body before rising to meet

my eyes. A knowing look of discovery and impatience and power—I can think of no better word—covered her face.

Turning, she slowly strolled from the bathroom, her hips swaying in her swimsuit. My instant arousal kept me in the bathroom until I could emerge without embarrassment.

I hurried to the church to serve mass. At communion Father Ed threw me a hard look when I placed my index finger to my lips to signal him that I would not receive. I knew he would cross-examine me later, so I would simply lead him to assume it was the same sin he had heard me confess every week or two for the last two years.

I stayed up late that night, well past midnight, and replayed the entire sequence of events on Badeen's property. Not because my conscience bothered me. Far from it. I was pleased and even calmly jubilant. Had the police known what I knew, and had they been able to prove what I knew, Badeen and Sinkhorn would have drawn the death penalty or, at the very least, life in prison. Because that proved impossible, I had achieved the same result, the just and moral result, if not the legal one.

My conscience was clear—at least, as clear as possible under the circumstances. I had removed two innately evil human beings from the face of the earth before they could harm Cari or anyone else. God had bequeathed them to the world. Now he could deal with them as he saw fit.

On the other hand, the grisly physical acts of murder, which were inherently abhorrent actions, birthed a revulsion in me that suffused my being.

In spite of the revulsion, I slept the sleep of the justified, if not of the innocent.

Chapter Thirty-One

The sky ruptured towards morning. A bombardment of thunder and lightning accompanied three inches of rain. I could not help wondering if I had caused a celebration in the heavens or a condemnation. Quite a naïve and egocentric thought, to say the least, but my imagination ran rampant in that vein for many hours on that day.

The rain continued intermittently the following day, surrendered to sunshine and wind the day after that, and revisited in sheets on the third day. By the fourth day, the squall line had passed. The Langs and I ate our evening meal with the local news droning from the small television on the kitchen counter.

"Police found the two men," the TV announcer said, *"after they failed to show up for work at the LaFarge Paper Plant for three days. They had last been seen on Friday night by several people at a local tavern. Authorities say they had been dead several days, perhaps since Saturday or Sunday, when found."*

A reporter appeared and spoke into the camera. *"I'm at the home of Virgil Badeen."*

The news camera panned to the pond. *"And that is where authorities found his body and that of Billy Sinkhorn."*

A moment later the same reporter faced the camera while standing on Sinkhorn's property. *"This is where Billy Sinkhorn resided until his recent death."*

The TV announcer appeared on screen. *"Police call the incidents bizarre."*

Pictures of Badeen and Sinkhorn flashed on the screen.

Cari gasped. "That's the man who asked directions to the QwikTrip!"

Mrs. Lang looked alarmed. "When?"

"Just a few days ago. Last week."

"Well, if he lived around here, you'd think he'd know where the QwikTrip is."

The reporter reappeared on the screen with Detective Gates.

"Detective Gates, have you ever seen anything like this?"

"No, I haven't."

"What do you think happened here?"

"We have a lot of work to do before we can even begin to speculate, but to find these two men, who were friends, dead at the same time goes beyond coincidence."

"Are you saying they were both murdered?"

"All I can say is, Sinkhorn was shot twice. There's no evidence of foul play with Badeen. It appears he drowned."

"Is it true Badeen's trousers were down when police found him?"

The detective hesitated before answering. *"I'd rather not comment on any physical findings until we've had a chance to fully investigate the crime scene and events prior to the incident. We do have some questions as to the nature of the relationship between the two men. Beyond that, I have no comment."*

"We've been told that Badeen's Doberman had to be subdued before anyone could come on the property. Does that rule out involvement of another party, or at least a third party that wasn't known by Badeen and his dog?"

"You're asking questions I'm neither able nor inclined to answer."

"We've seen bloodhounds. Have they picked up anything?"

"Not yet. The rain these last few days has probably washed away any scent that might have been left."

Thunder rolled outside. Mrs. Lang turned off the television. "I've had enough to last me a lifetime. Such a nice quiet town and now this."

"Maybe the town is better off now," I said.

Cari leveled a killing glare at me. "Jason!"

158

"He might have a point," said Mr. Lang. "I heard those two were real lowlifes."

"You can't go around killing people, Dad."

"She's right, Harold. That's what the law is for."

"What if the law doesn't work?" I said.

Gathering up the plates, Mrs. Lang looked at me sharply. "Do we want people running around taking the law into their own hands? Pretty soon nobody'd be safe, including us. I'm going to listen to some music. Lawrence Welk would sure hit the spot right now."

Cari rolled her eyes. Mr. Lang nodded absently and drank his coffee.

Chapter Thirty-Two

Cari and I rode our bikes late in the afternoon on the following Sunday after supper. We rode into town, pedaled past Freepont High, the softball diamonds in Mead Park, down Main Street, and up Stephens. Ice cream cones beckoned at the Unified Dairy. Mr. Elber always scooped up extra big dips for us when he was working. Vanilla for me, banana for Cari.

After the ice cream, Cari suggested that we ride out to Park Land golf course to hit some range balls.

"Why? We don't even play golf."

"It's fun. A bunch of us girls hit balls last week. I hit some good ones for a beginner."

"Okay."

On the way, we had to pass Calvary Cemetery where I worked with Mr. Bensen.

"Let's go through the graveyard," she said.

"I see enough of that place during the week." I didn't think it necessary to mention that my father was buried there.

"Oh, come on! There aren't any ghosts."

She turned in and I followed. The narrow road formed a long U-shaped loop into the cemetery and back out. When we had ridden three-quarters of the way around, Cari veered off to the right. She walked her bike well away from the road to a secluded area beneath large pine trees along the west fence.

"What's the deal?" I asked.

"I'm tired. Let's take a break."

We sat on the soft grass near the pine trees with the breeze whispering through the branches and around the old-fashioned grave stones, some of which stood seven or eight feet high.

Huge, billowy clouds, their tips glowing from the setting

sun, floated overhead in the pre-twilight. Late summer ripeness lent a pleasant redolence to the cool air. The warm grass served as a perfect blanket between us and the cool earth.

"That one looks like a pair of big boobs," she said.

Her comment excited me. To mask my arousal, I laughed and said, "You have a creative imagination."

"Don't you see them?"

"Yeah, kind of, I guess."

We lay back and watched the clouds until dusk. Cari, talkative as ever, chattered about everything and nothing. After a while I didn't feel like talking or listening.

"Something wrong?" she asked.

"Notice how the birds sing differently this time of day? How everything changes when the world transitions from day to night?"

"You're a wonderful conversationalist, Ferris, just brilliant. You pick up the thread and move right along. Do you practice that or what?"

My hand found hers at my side and gripped it tightly. She turned to me and immediately rolled onto her side. "You're crying!" she said. "What is it? What's wrong?"

"Oh, Cari! Everything is wrong. Everything! Dear God!"

I sobbed uncontrollably. Cari lay across my chest and cradled my face in her hands.

"Tell me what's wrong!"

"I need to hold you, Cari. God, how I need to hold you!"

"What is it?"

My arms encircled her as she straddled me. We kissed, gently at first, then deeply. My hands slid down beyond the small of her back. I pressed her to my body. When she arched against me, I rolled her onto her back and lay on top of her. Her half-closed eyes conveyed magical wonder, her parted lips seductiveness.

"Let me touch you?" she whispered.

"I want you to!"

Her hand slid beneath the elastic waistband of my briefs.

"Cari, we shouldn't—we can't—oh God!"

A minute later, I half-rose, shuddering and gasping, before I felt the hot semen on my belly and her hand still moving on me. I collapsed on her, rigid, wanting her more than anything else in the world, feeling both empty and filled—*fulfilled*—and wishing I could stay there forever.

"It's okay, it's okay," she said in a soothing voice.

I kissed her nose, her eyes, cheeks, forehead, lips. Her damp skin was warm and welcoming.

"You'll always be my secret girl. I'm so sad we won't be together."

"Please don't say that. Not now."

I shook my head and placed my index finger to her lips. I leaned on my elbow. "Let me see you naked. Just this once. I'll never in my life look at another girl naked."

After a slight hesitation, she tugged at the snaps of her halter. When it dropped away from her breasts, my breath left me. I felt lightheaded.

"Take off my panties."

On my knees I hooked my fingers under the waistband of her shorts.

"You have to unbutton them," she said.

She shifted her weight to one hip to show me the button and zipper. I trembled so badly I could hardly undo the button. The zipper opened more easily. She rose up so I could pull her shorts down. Only her panties remained.

I leaned over and kissed her on the lips before slowly sliding the panties over her hips, down her thighs, over her knees and ankles. Her legs together, she lay naked before me in a revelation so lovely, so overwhelming, so *beatific,* I could hardly stand it.

"You are so beautiful!"

Bracing myself on the palms of my hands, I hovered over her and kissed her breasts before lowering myself onto her, my cheek next to hers, and whispering into her ear. "Eve couldn't have been more perfect."

"Kiss me?" It wasn't really a question.

My chest wanted to burst. I kissed her, then pushed myself up. "You have to save yourself."

"I want it to be you."

"Cari—"

"Don't get up yet. Please don't."

"Okay, just for a minute."

We kissed again, this time without end. I felt her hand on me, felt her move her pelvis and spread her legs slightly. As I tentatively penetrated her, I felt for the first time what a man is born to feel, something I had never felt before but had imagined countless times. The first time is no doubt unique. She gasped and we both began to thrust instinctively as human beings have since the dawn of our species without instruction or thought or sense of right or wrong. It took only minutes before the same sensation I had felt moments earlier spread over and through me like a hot sensory riptide. Using every ounce of my willpower, I pulled away.

"No, don't take—don't leave—keep it—"

"If I don't, I won't. Ever. And you can't get pregnant," I managed to tell her through my heavy breathing. I wasn't feeling very articulate.

"Just hold me a while."

"Let's get dressed first."

"You mean let *me* get dressed. You're not undressed." She laughed at the look on my face. Her laugh, so natural, so unaffected and symptomatic of her personality, released the emotional tension of the moment. I loved her even more than I had only seconds before.

I picked up her panties and started pushing them up her legs. When she arched up to help me, I noticed a bead of perspiration midway between her belly button and her vagina. It caught a faint ray of light and glistened against her skin. A thought struck me: *How pure! How symbolic its location between the vestige of her birth and the portal of new life.*

My memory no doubt embellishes the brief moment in order to capture the feeling. Be that as it may, I inclined my head and buried my face between her legs, where her scent and her softness and her verbal ejaculations nearly sent me into an epiphanic delirium.

I stayed there until I realized I had to stop or my life

would veer off in a direction that scared me because it was so foreign to what I had always planned to do. Her panties somehow ended up at her midriff.

"Do my top, too."

I fumbled and bumbled with the snaps, all thumbs, still shaking. Finished, I tucked in my shirt. I embraced her when we got to our feet. We stayed that way for many minutes—not nearly long enough.

"I wish this could last an eternity," I said to her.

"You never told me what's wrong."

"It's better now."

"You won't tell me about it?"

"No."

We held each other in the cool quietude of the dying day.

"Do you ever see another girl?"

I cupped her face in my hands and shook my head. "You're the only girl I'll ever want."

"I'm not a girl. I'm a woman now."

"A perfect woman."

I meant it then and I still mean it.

Chapter Thirty-Three

The days and weeks passed slowly. The anti-climactic calm threw me into a state of limbo, cut off from a former life in so many ways, my parents gone, my adolescence at an end.

While trying to preserve my worldview—not the word I would have used at the time—I had enough presence of mind to realize that I no longer saw the world through a clear lens, but through a prism that refracted reality into infinite combinations and possibilities. Life had gone from simple to complex to truly byzantine.

For whatever reason, I wanted to see my mother for the first time since her confinement. I asked for and received permission to visit her. Father Ed drove me.

I stood on the sidewalk across the street from the state hospital, which looked uglier and more foreboding than I recalled. I didn't want to go in. I did want to see her and wanted to know firsthand whether she had progressed since that night I had found her naked in the road in front of our home.

When they led me to her room, she sat on a wooden chair in a well-lit, essentially featureless room with heavy grating on the solitary window. Her eyes were dark and lifeless. She looked even gaunter than I remembered. She was happy to see me. We hugged and she remarked how tall I had become. In her deluded state, she may have remembered me as a small boy.

"Are you a priest yet?"

"Not yet. I'm so glad to see you, Mom."

"I'm getting a lot better."

"You come home as soon as you can."

"How's your father? Is he still working so hard? Does he

take you fishing?"

I started to lie, to say yes, we go fishing all the time, Mom. Perhaps I should have but I didn't. "He's in heaven, remember?"

Her next words nearly destroyed me.

"Oh, you know what a trickster he is," she said. "One of these days he'll poke his head through the door and say, 'Fish are biting, Jason. Let's go!'"

I embraced her—what else could I do?—and told her I'd return soon, a shameful statement that I recognized as a lie the moment I said it.

"You rest and get strong, Mom." Those were my last words to her that day. I returned to see her when I could. Which, I'm ashamed to say, was infrequently.

A new layer of sadness joined the one from my father's death. I hoped and believed that time would assuage my grief, which it has indeed done. However, something also told me their deaths had instilled in me an essential and all-encompassing sense of loss that would transcend any possible emotional amelioration the passage of time could bestow. This has also proved to be true.

The visit increased my determination to enter the priesthood, for my mother and in memory of her happier times, and maybe to escape the reality of my own contorted life. On the ride home with Father Ed, I pleaded my case.

"Father, I need you to help me get into a prep seminary this fall."

"The Church considers very few young men before they complete high school."

"You know I've always wanted to be a priest. Maybe the Church could be a little flexible. There'll be some money when the house sells and from the life insurance. I need you to go to bat for me."

"I'll see what I can do."

Shortly after my conversation with Father Ed, the Langs and I gathered for supper. As usual, they had the TV on. The anchorman announced the following: *Another twist tonight in the strange case of Virgil Badeen and Billy Sinkhorn. You may*

166

recall the authorities found them both dead in a pond on Badeen's property. Authorities earlier revealed that Badeen's gun had killed Sinkhorn.

"A pathology report now confirms that Badeen did not die from drowning as previously believed. It turns out that Badeen, who was highly allergic to bee venom, so allergic that the sting of only one bee could kill him, had gone into anaphylactic shock from multiple bee stings. He may have entered the water to escape the bees. His tongue had swollen so badly that it would have been impossible for him to breathe. Therefore, there was no water in his lungs. An ironic footnote to a bizarre case. In other news...."

Cari dropped her fork and stared at me in stunned recognition. She pushed back from the table and ran from the room under the dumbfounded gaze of her parents. I followed.

We rode our bikes for miles without saying a word. We ended up at Augustine High where we laid our bikes on the football field and sat on the bleachers. I decided to let Cari take the lead. She didn't engage in any small talk.

"Your bees killed that man."

"They sting when they get riled up."

"But why?"

"They murdered that man at LaFarge Paper. Dumped him into the pulp tank."

"How do you know that? And even so—"

"I know because my father is dead."

She studied me in the gathering gloom. "Your dad saw what happened?"

"They forced him to watch. Mr. Pell too. Do you think Pell died accidentally while fishing? Why do you think my father committed suicide?"

"God, Jason!"

Neither of us said anything for several moments in the enveloping dusk. Here and there a night sound pierced the gloom.

"Listen," I said, "the day creatures have given way to the night ones. The stalked and the stalkers. The night hides all of it from us."

She remained silent, no doubt trying to process the events of the summer and trying to comprehend what they all meant. No easy task. I'd had weeks and months to ruminate, and I still struggled for answers. Everything had hit her at once.

"I keep wishing this is a bad dream that will end when I wake up. How can you still be a priest?"

"The world's a better place now."

"I thought I knew you."

"I'm sorry you have to carry what you think you know."

"Cut it, Jason. You're starting to scare me. Like you don't even know what's real anymore."

"I never want anything bad for you."

She began to cry. It was almost more than I could bear. I held her.

"It's okay, Cari. Let it come out."

"For God's sake, Jason, you don't want me in your life, you go and kill those men—what's happening to us?"

She broke away and ran to the end of the bleacher section, where she vomited. I handed her my handkerchief and held her again while we sat on the bleachers. She calmed down after a minute or two.

"I'm sorry you know. I never wanted you to know. I should have denied everything."

"I would have found out. I know you. It's so crazy. When we made love in the cemetery, it was so beautiful. I can still feel it, can still feel you. And now that seems like another life in another dimension."

We struggled to our feet and stood there holding each other as darkness surrounded us. I had the feeling during those few sacred minutes that the world had left us alone, that nothing else mattered or ever could matter.

"This will change our lives forever," she said. "We will live strange lives."

"It's what we do from now on that matters."

"Maybe so. We have to keep living. Now the future scares me."

The next day Detective Pearson paid me a surprise visit.

She told me she had just gotten off duty, happened to be driving by, and decided to see how I was doing—as if I believed her.

We sat on the front porch as the sun slanted across the yard with just enough breeze blowing to keep the mosquitoes at bay. After some small talk, she got down to the real reason for her visit.

"You heard the latest news about those two guys who worked with your dad?"

"It was on TV earlier."

"Pretty weird deal, huh?"

I nodded. She sat there slowly running her tongue back and forth over her lower lip and gazing across the road where Clem Ferguson tended his bees. An attractive woman, she toiled in what I chauvinistically thought was a male occupation.

"Goes beyond weird. I mean, the physical evidence showed Sinkhorn was in the water when he got shot. The rains had washed away the blood, but pieces of skull and brains were still on the ground at the edge of the pond."

When I said nothing, she continued. "I've never quite figured out how Badeen could have shot him, busy as he was fighting off the bees. With his pants down, to boot. I suppose he could have shot Sinkhorn before the bees just happened along and decided to lunch on him. Then again, if he wasn't trying to escape from the bees, why was he in the water? Why would both of them be in the water? And if bees were attacking him, why would he re-holster his pistol after shooting Sinkhorn? How incredible is that?"

Although I didn't want to be rude, something told me it was a good time to keep my mouth shut.

"What a case. I mean, crazy. Know what we found in Badeen's outhouse—speaking of which, he must have been some kind of loony, don't you think? Had indoor plumbing that he apparently didn't use much. Wanted to be rustic, I suppose. Anyway, we found blobs of honey and some dead bees in his outhouse. That honey made no sense. Still doesn't."

I swallowed hard and felt sweat on the back of my neck.

The detective never took her eyes off me.

"Bees do a lot of good," she said. "I mean, they give us honey, they pollinate crops for farmers, and who knows what else. Ever wondered how people got them to hive in the first place?"

"No, ma'am."

She ran her hand through her hair. "We think we're so smart today with all our technology, but people back then were smart too. Pretty darn creative, don't you think, getting bees to work for us?"

"Yes, ma'am."

"Know much about them?"

"A little." I pointed across the road. "Mr. Ferguson lets me help once in a while."

"You don't say. Ever been stung?"

I nodded. She slid off the porch step and brushed her slacks with her hands.

"Good thing you're not allergic like some people."

She stared at me in a peculiar manner and held me in her gaze. I thought I detected the barest shadow of a smile. Perhaps I imagined it.

"Guess I'm lucky," I said.

"Very lucky." She again peered at me as if she were trying to piece together a puzzle or already had. "Well, I have to run. See you around, Jason."

She shook my hand and walked at a measured pace to her car. She gazed across the road a long time, then at me, before she got into her car and drove off.

Chapter Thirty-Four

2007

Monsignor Korth struggled up from his pillow and braced himself on his elbows. Perspiration beaded his forehead. His breathing was labored and raspy. He stared past Jason into the dark recesses of the room.

"Good God, man! Two murders on your head! And although you choked up a few times, you told it so dispassionately."

"It's ancient history. I have no remorse."

"None at all?"

"None. I believe our God will deal justly with them and perhaps ultimately with mercy, but I hope for a long time they are in Dante's seventh ring in a river of boiling blood, riddled by centaur arrows every time they seek a moment's relief."

"You are a man without feeling."

"On the contrary, what I did gives rise to a violent disgust nearly every day of my life. At times I feel the urge to vomit and actually have on occasion. Like any taking of life, the killings were innately and undeniably repugnant. Grisly.

"I must deal with those aspects of it. At the end of the day, my reason takes over, and I feel no pity for Badeen and Sinkhorn."

"Where is your pastoral charity?"

"With all due respect, Monsignor, have you no pity for the two men they murdered? No pity for my parents? For the innocent girl who would have been the next victim? Does the Church, like our courts, write off the victims and extend compassion only to the perpetrators?

"There are two possibilities regarding the men I killed.

Either God created them that way or they had free will and chose to kill and hurt people. In either case I carried out my human responsibility. Their eternal fate is God's business and not my concern."

The monsignor's chest heaved. His head swung from side to side as if he could not believe what he had heard.

"Did you ever once think of seeking absolution?"

Jason faced Korth squarely. "I've tried sporadically and half-heartedly for over twenty years to be sorry. Sorrow never comes and probably never will. With God as my witness, I'm sorry I had to do it, but not that I did it. That's the most honest statement I can make.

"In fact, I lie to myself and to you when I say I've tried to be sorry. My attempts at sorrow are exercises in self-deception, perhaps to gain some nebulous degree of relief. There's no denying that I long for the relief the confessional always afforded before I murdered. But I will never be sorry I killed those two men."

"Vigilante justice. Dear Christ! Without contrition there can't be absolution."

"My actions saved at least one life. I view them as perfect acts of sin prevention."

Korth began to cough. Deep gasps and a peculiar rattling punctuated his coughing. His face turned crimson. Jason quickly poured water into a glass and offered it to him, curling his arm around the monsignor's shoulders and holding the glass to his lips to help him drink. Korth took a few small sips before he waved the water away. Jason set the glass on the tray and sat down.

"No, sir! They were *im*perfect acts!" The monsignor's fist pounded the edge of his bed. "What you say is illusory. Nothing we do remains separate from our other actions. How can you expect to continue your vocation with this on your soul?"

"By act of will. I don't allow their blood to provoke my conscience."

Korth fell back on his pillow and closed his eyes. "You feel you stand on principle. Are you sure it's not pride?"

Jason had discarded the thought countless times over the years. He didn't reply to the monsignor's astute question.

"Our ancient adversary is most cunning. He knows infinite ways of preying on us with subtle infusions of pride, infusions we may not even recognize for what they are."

Eyes still closed, Korth went silent. He opened his eyes and turned to face Jason. "I can't allow you to become the next spiritual director of this college."

Jason vaulted from his chair. "With all due respect, Monsignor, my spiritual state does not compromise the sacraments I dispense as a priest. Nor does it invalidate my advice and counsel as a spiritual guide."

Korth threw his hands up. "Please don't lecture me on sacramental efficacy! And don't get legalistic. We both know the issues here. Can a cowardly officer lead brave troops? Can a false prophet lead his flock? Not for long. Truth has a way of coming out of hiding sooner or later.

"Query: What do you feel when you celebrate mass, especially when you consecrate the bread and wine? How can you presume to perform such a sacred act with such a blackened soul?"

Jason had never seen the monsignor so agitated or so tired-looking.

"Monsignor, since you bring up consecration, allow me to tell you one more thing. The first time I celebrated mass, I thought of Cari when I consecrated the bread and wine. And almost every time since. That's not to say I'm not awed by the act of consecration. I am. To the point of being overwhelmed at times. But the emotion I experienced that day among the tombstones with Cari was the most intense religious epiphany I'll ever experience. True 'at-one-ment', if you will. Which I never confessed. Because it was pure and redemptive."

"Oh please. Puppy love the most religious ... whatever. Your very words are a profanation, a self-deception. Pour me a finger of that Scotch."

Jason poured a half-jigger. Korth sipped the liquor, then tipped the glass and drained it. He wearily motioned for Jason to take the glass.

"I haven't confessed for another reason. How would you feel hearing such a confession? The murders had no element of self-defense. Badeen wanted me to live with the knowledge of what had happened. He knew it was the cruelest thing he could do to me.

"Would you grant absolution? Would you direct me to civil authority? How would you feel about me as a person and servant of God from then on? What would you think whenever you saw me in the dining hall or at the altar or in a faculty meeting? If you granted absolution, would you go to God confident of your own salvation?"

"What a vile legacy for the students of this school if your past ever came to light. Even as an alternative to scandal, I would not absolve you. You are blasphemous. You commit grave sacrilege every time you consecrate, every time you receive our Lord's body and blood."

He dropped back onto his pillow and closed his eyes, as if gathering his strength. When he opened his eyes and began speaking, he stared at the ceiling while his words ripped into Jason with the unrelenting force of a power auger.

"This discussion leads nowhere and has no ultimate substance. Your ordination was not valid. You had committed voluntary homicide, which is a permanent impediment to receiving the sacrament of Holy Orders. *Impedimenta perpetua.* The Code of Canon Law uses the euphemistic word 'irregularity.' Whatever the semantics, you are permanently precluded from exercising the orders received."

"I don't believe God would withhold His grace from flowing through me to the recipients of the sacraments I administer."

"I don't know the answer to that. I do know that you showed gross disrespect for our Church and our God when you fraudulently received Holy Orders. Only the Apostolic See can provide dispensation from a perpetual irregularity so as to allow ordination—and such dispensation is, I assure you, extremely difficult to secure. You never even so much as sought absolution from a parish priest! What were you thinking?"

174

Jason drank the last of his Scotch. He set his glass down, not certain what to say. Monsignor Korth gazed at him, waiting, not about to let him off the hook.

"I had wanted to become a priest all my life. I believed with all my heart I would be a good one. I committed to obedience and celibacy, which I've observed strictly. Granted, I may chip at the edges of obedience when I challenge some of the Church's precepts, but when my faith confronts my reason, I usually allow or force faith to supersede my intellect. I believe I've been a loyal disciple of Holy Mother Church, and a good teacher."

"Stop right there. How can you possibly say you've been obedient? You violently disobeyed the Canon by receiving Holy Orders when you had no moral or procedural right to them. Your ordination was a sham, totally false and deceitful. A lie!"

"I defer to you, Monsignor. I can't dispute the facts. I've always felt justified in what I did because I saw no other way to defend an innocent human being. A human being whom I just so happened to love and admire and respect."

"You have to realize that Badeen, if your narrative was accurate, did not say he would kill your friend. You *assumed* that's what he meant and that he would follow through with it."

Heat shot up Jason's neck. "A damned good assumption, Monsignor, given his track record. What would you have assumed?"

"I can't speculate. Allow me to digress. I'm curious as to your method. You took a great risk with your assassin bees—which, by the way, you stole from your neighbor."

Tired of the dialogue, Jason took a deep breath and calmed himself.

"I did steal the bees, but when my parents' affairs were settled, I put fifty dollars in Mr. Ferguson's mailbox late one night.

"Risky assassins? Yes and no. I did have the pistol as a backup, but had the bees failed, Badeen probably would have killed me, given his strength and prowess with a handgun.

However, as scared as I was, I also felt confident that I had an edge on him. I knew his habits and his one vulnerability.

"The first time I saw the pouch he wore at his waist, I thought it was a purse. It struck me as odd. Why would a mountain of a man like that wear a purse? I had no idea what the word EpiPen on the pouch meant. My research in the library informed me that Badeen had to be highly allergic. But allergic to what? That was a problem.

"The more I thought about it, the more I narrowed it down to insect bites or bee stings rather than a food product. I came to that conclusion because he always had that pouch on him, even when he chopped wood. I could have been wrong. In that case, I hoped the bees would provide enough distraction to give me time to use my pistol.

"My problem lay in figuring out how to get him stung. Mr. Ferguson and further research solved that problem. You see, when a honeybee stings, its barbed stinger rips from its body and releases potent alarm pheromones that excite all nearby bees into a defensive state, meaning they attack. It doesn't even take a sting to excite them. The mere presence of danger will cause a release of alarm pheromones. The loss of a stinger heightens the release and the response.

"One of the most important pheromones released is isopentyl acetate, also known as isoamyl acetate. The "banana oil" I got at the dairy wasn't banana oil at all. It was isoamyl acetate, a synthetic substance used in flavorings, perfumes, and numerous other items, including paints and varnishes.

"When I sprinkled the hive with the oil, the scent instantly turned the bees into aggressive killers. As an added precaution, I shook the hive before throwing it at Badeen. I hoped the shaking would frighten the bees into a killing frenzy.

"I knew at least one of them would sting the man. As it turned out, they probably stung him dozens of times. He never stood a chance."

"Good God in heaven! Only a depraved, diabolic mind could even—" Korth closed his eyes. "The woman. Do you still see her?"

"We've kept in touch off and on. It has always been strictly platonic. I hadn't seen her for two years until my mother's funeral yesterday."

"Tell me about that."

Chapter Thirty-Five

Last week when I received word of my mother's death, I called the Freepont Funeral Home to initiate arrangements. I told them I would say mass and forgo a reception.

My mother had been institutionalized for twenty years, so few people remembered her. Even so, a handful of her classmates showed up at the wake, as did our next-door neighbors, the Langs, whom I took to dinner the evening before the requiem.

Cari still lived in Minneapolis following her divorce, and she played in the Minneapolis Symphony. They didn't know whether she'd be able to make it back for the funeral.

I found it difficult to concentrate on the mass because I kept watching for her. Much to my dismay, she never showed up at the church. Only four mourners attended the graveside rites. Nature provided a fairly warm, sunny day, but the glare from the snow was blinding.

A beige car inched down the narrow cemetery road as I concluded final prayers. Cari had arrived. I wrapped things up and told the funeral director he could leave. I didn't want another ride in a hearse anyway. He left and I joined Cari.

I threw my arms around her. "It's so good to see you! I feared you weren't coming. You look terrific!"

"Bad, bad accident on the interstate. We sat for two hours waiting for them to clear the wreckage."

"Shall we take a short walk?"

She nodded with enthusiasm and we struck off through the cemetery. I asked her if she had taken a vow of silence after her divorce. She laughed as only she can.

"After a marriage from hell, I wasn't taking a chance on any kind of vow."

"I hated him through your letters."

"That's all in the past. The symphony finally hired me full-time. And two months ago I met a really sweet guy."

My anticipation evaporated. She caught the look on my face and smiled to cover up. "Please be happy for me?"

"I always want you to be happy."

She squeezed my hand to get through the moment. "What have you been up to?"

"When they called to tell me my mother had died, I immediately thought I might see you. Are you going to marry him?"

She shrugged dismissively. "You're way ahead of me."

"Are you intimate?"

"Please don't, Jason."

She was disappointed in me and becoming impatient. I blundered on.

"If I weren't a priest, would there be anything for us?"

Her steady gaze searched my face. When I touched her arm, she stiffened ever so slightly. She began to say something but hesitated. Instead, she took my hand and we resumed walking.

"So many times over the years I've thought of you that way—in part, I suppose, because of 'first love syndrome' or whatever. But now…"

"Is he committed to you?"

"He has some baggage. I mean, he's working through some things that will take awhile."

"Cari, it's me. No code, okay?"

"He's married. I mean, the marriage is over, but it's not ended. Their kids...his job..."

"He'll never end it."

She jerked her hand from mine and faced me. "God damn it, Jason! I don't need this!"

Her vehemence took me aback. I touched her cheek.

"Forgive my stupid remark. Look, I can see you're cold. Let's go somewhere. I noticed Ganova's is still in business."

Her eyes still blazing, she nodded her acceptance of my suggestion. At that moment, as if telepathically, we both

179

realized that we stood only a few rows of tombstones away from where we had lost our virginity so many years earlier. We walked to her car in silence.

Ganova's had become a secondary hangout after a pizza place, Tarce's, had closed. The kids of the original owner now ran the place.

We found a corner booth at the restaurant, sat nearly side-by-side, and ordered two beers from a waitress who appeared to be salivating over an impending scandal involving a priest and a lovely woman. She hovered across the room, pretending she wasn't watching but in fact wasn't missing anything going on in our booth. The place was busy enough, thank goodness, to keep our conversation relatively private.

Cari nodded at the brass violin on my lapel and asked, "Do I recognize your pin?"

"I converted it when I began wearing suits."

She smiled. "Well, conversions are in your line of work. Sorry for my little tantrum back there."

"I had it coming. More important, you so much as said I'm in your life. Do you have any idea how special that makes me feel?"

"I knew you'd be a kinky priest."

We both laughed at the old refrain. Then I said something I'll never forget. "I think of you constantly. Have for months. Years. All my life. I need you as much as I need God. Maybe more."

She searched my face. "How long can you be gone?"

The waitress approached. "You folks care for another?"

I told her not yet. Smirking, she stared at my collar before she sashayed across the floor with an exaggerated swing of her backside.

"Cari, our annual retreat begins in four days. I'm down to the last-minute crunching."

She leaned back. "All so hypothetical anyway." She reached for the check. I gripped her wrist.

"They depend on me. May I call you?"

"What's the point? You could never leave the priesthood. Not completely. We both know that. I can't say I want you to."

She smiled impishly. "Besides, men never call."

I placed my hand over hers. The waitress would be the hands-down star at her next gossip session.

"You're thinking I could never abandon my vows, never fully commit. Ironically, I've had that kind of problem with my vocation. I've always been on the outside looking in since that summer."

Her expression told me she had no idea what I meant.

"I never confessed the murders."

"God, Jason! You've always—I know how important confession is to you. How can you be a priest? I mean—"

Neither of us knew what to say. She broke the impasse by reaching into her purse and bringing out a bright yellow Post-It pad on which she wrote her phone number. She slid it across the table to me.

"If you ever need to talk."

"There's one thing I need to know. Did you—have you ever forgiven me for what I did?"

She covered my hand with hers. "Of course I did. A long time ago."

"I can't begin to tell you how much that means to me. Can we stay in touch?"

"I hope we will."

Chapter Thirty-Six

Monsignor Korth's appearance had deteriorated. Looking drained of all strength, he stared at Jason through dull eyes—eyes that an hour earlier had been alert and piercing.

"That's my story, Monsignor. I've withheld nothing."

"I'll say this: You're a man of your word. When you said you'd provide ample detail, you meant it. More than I needed, especially the salacious aspects. Your vocation, such as it is, is in serious jeopardy—and that's the least of your worries. You're in love with a woman, a divorced one at that. I wish I could help you."

"She's the finest woman I've ever met. She has matured into a well-rounded, sensible person. If she were a practicing Catholic, she'd be consigned to a life of aloneness simply because she had married someone who turned into an abusive monster. I don't think that makes sense.

"The Church's position on divorce is uncharitable and often barbaric. The evasive, legalistic machinery of annulment is hypocritical, worthy of the Scribes and Pharisees. It has devolved into a derisive joke—not entirely warranted, but not entirely unwarranted, either."

"You say this woman is so wonderful. I don't know her, of course, but from what you've told me, I don't see her that way. Are you sure she's not your fantasy, a fantasy the years have magnified?

"Be that as it may, let me offer some advice: Before you take on too many of the Church's issues, you'd better consider your own. Getting Rome's dispensation from validly conferred Holy Orders is an arduous process. I don't know the process for—how shall I say it?—*retracting* invalid orders. What a mess you've created."

"The Church teaches, and I've always believed, that the sacrament of ordination confers an indelible spiritual character on the recipient. That a priest can't, strictly speaking, become a layman again. He's marked permanently."

"True in the case of a valid conferment. Yours completely invalid." Korth's face flushed. He sat partially upright and started coughing. An awful gasping rattle followed. He tried to raise his left arm. It flopped limply onto the bed. His head tilted left on the pillow.

"Monsignor!" Jason bent over and cradled him in his arms. "Say something!" He shook him gently. "Oh God, Joe! Don't die! Please!" *What have I done?*

Faculty members and students had crowded around the dormitory entrance by the time Jason emerged from the building with the paramedics wheeling Monsignor Korth out on a gurney. Flashing lights from the ambulance and fire department life squad vehicle caromed off buildings and trees and cars. The cold gusty wind swirled through the assemblage as the paramedics rolled the gurney into the rear of the ambulance and closed the doors. The vehicle pulled away with its siren wailing. Nick Beck, a priest and brilliant chemist who had attended Augustine High School, approached Jason.

"I understand you were with him, Jason."

"Yes."

"What a blessing he wasn't alone. It had to be hard for you."

"His courage amazed me. I pray he lives."

"Courage?"

"Incredible courage. And damn it, I never called him Joe until it was too late. Excuse me, Nick. It's been a long night."

"Sure. Catch you later."

The first floor of Duquesne Hall housed the college's administrative offices. Jason had scant reason to go there often, although, of course, he knew each office and its occupants, including secretaries and other staffers.

Today, three days after Monsignor Korth's stroke, the

spotless, highly polished condition of the place impressed Jason, as it always did, and generated a mild surge of institutional pride. The corridor's shiny terrazzo floor exaggerated his footfalls in the deserted building.

He paused to read the bronze plaque on the partially opened door: Lawrence Casek, President. Ten o'clock at night and the only person still working was the president. Jason knocked on the door.

"Come in."

The president, a slender, nattily dressed layman in his late forties who had been a terrific point guard in his youth, bounded to the door as Jason entered.

"Thanks so much for coming at this hour, Father. Please have a chair. Here, let me take your coat." He motioned Jason to a sofa.

The college's gold and maroon colors tastefully accented the office, including the president's tie, which still looked crisp and snug at his throat when he joined Jason on the sofa.

"May I get you a drink, Father?"

"No thank you, sir. I'm fine."

"Coke? Juice?"

"Nothing, thanks."

"You were close to the monsignor."

"We've worked together many years."

"He spoke most highly of you."

"Shouldn't we speak in present tense?"

Casek flushed. "Please forgive me. However, his chances of recovering from such a massive stroke are slender. Three days in a coma don't bode well."

He gathered himself and continued with conviction.

"Your healthy irreverence is very valuable to this college. I want you to be the next spiritual director. The faculty supports you. The students would follow you off a cliff. Do you accept?"

Jason found himself unable to answer.

"Father?"

"It's premature. The monsignor is still the director."

Visibly taken aback and upset, Casek nodded.

"I understand. We'll talk at a more appropriate time."

"Thank you."

Casek wasn't ready to dismiss Jason quite yet. He leaned forward on the edge of the sofa when he spoke.

"Father, assuming the monsignor doesn't make it, I want his successor to take the position to the next level. I know what's out there. I thought things were bad years ago when I flew jets for the Navy. They're worse now.

"Our young men and women need moral leadership like never before. Not ivory tower stuff. Real-world leadership with guts and brains. We need to ramp up the spirituality of this institution."

He all but catapulted himself from the sofa and returned from his desk a moment later with a manila folder.

"I've reviewed your file. You've been in a religious setting since high school. On the surface, you don't have any—shall we say—street experience. My gut tells me you have the savvy to go along with your intelligence and moral fiber, that you could confront evil head-on and deal with it. Am I right?"

"I like to think so."

"Long story short, I'd expect you to pour everything you have into the job. This student body will reflect nothing short of the highest Christian ideals. Am I clear?"

Jason managed to nod his understanding.

"Good."

Casek arose, shook Jason's hand, and helped him on with his coat.

"You have my full support, Father, whatever you decide. And by the way, I'm a man who appreciates loyalty. Your loyalty to Monsignor Korth impresses me."

"Thank you, sir."

It seemed colder when he stepped out onto the east porch of Duquesne Hall. He looked up into the deep, starless sky and remembered Monsignor Korth's words: *Can a cowardly officer lead brave troops? Can a false prophet lead his flock? Is it principle or pride?*

A blast of wind drew him back to the present. If only the

wind could carry away the stain of human blood, the blood of two evil men and one holy man, for he was convinced that he had caused the stroke that would soon kill the monsignor, a death that would torment him until the day of his own.

He descended the steps at the south end of Duquesne Hall and rounded the corner of the building to the public sidewalk that stretched down the long hill into the dim distance toward Beckman Hall. The ten-foot-high bronze statue of Saint Victor, arm raised in benediction, loomed over him.

What are the benchmarks of bravery? How do we define false and genuine? Are the definitions the same in all circumstances? Does context have bearing? What meaning do the answers have? How can we know them?

Jason drew the collar of his coat snugly against his throat. Too many questions, not enough answers. He leaned into the biting wind and hurried to the refuge of his apartment.

Chapter Thirty-Seven

His thoughts remained in disarray when he reached the warm haven of his apartment. He hung up his coat and reached for his father's old Army bugle that hung from a nail on the life-size crucifix in the middle of the room. Handling the bugle had always calmed him over the years and served to bring things into perspective—why he had done what he had, why he believed as he did, why he had to forge ahead on the path he had committed to. Would it work this time?

He replaced the bugle and reached for the yellow Post-It on his desk with Cari's number. Although he had considered transferring her number to a more permanent location, such as his cell phone or desk calendar, he could not bring himself to do so. She had touched the Post-It and written her number on it. He viewed it as a relic of sorts, something physical that linked him to her and to their last conversation. It had been an easy decision to keep the Post-It.

He removed his Roman collar and laid it alongside Cari's phone number. Drumming his left fingers on the slip of paper while still touching the collar with his right hand, he had a long Hamlet moment before he arose to go to bed.

Sleep proved illusive. He tossed and turned, lay awake, and repeatedly checked the time on the alarm clock. He flung the covers back at three-thirty, swung his feet to the floor, and picked up his cell phone.

She answered on the fourth ring, the sleep in her voice unmistakable.

"Cari? Jason. I need to see you. I can be there in four hours."

"Are you okay? Is something wrong?"

"Everything is fine."

"Mind telling me what's going on? Jeez, Jason, it's three-thirty in the bleeping morning."

"I can't explain over the phone. May I come up?"

"You really are a kinky priest. Of course you can come, but you have to buy me breakfast."

"You're on. Thanks. I'll call for directions when I get close. Bye."

He dressed in civvies, threw on a warm jacket, and rushed to the door. He backtracked. Lifting his Roman collar from his desk, he hung it on the crucifix to replace the bugle, which he took with him.

She invited him in but agreed to his suggestion to take a walk in a park he had passed a few blocks from her apartment.

The pale sun shone through early morning clouds as they walked hand-in-hand down a path bordering a lagoon. Frost covered everything with a layer of pristine whiteness and even floated in the sparkling air.

No doubt wondering why he'd come, she waited for him to explain. Not at all sure how to begin, he decided to plunge right in.

"I'm going to ask for dispensation from my vows," he said and embraced her. "I love you and need you in my life." She looked nonplussed. He tightened his embrace. "One step at a time, nothing taken for granted."

She pulled away from him. "Since the funeral, I've thought about you—us—a lot. I mean, every day. And…"

"And?"

"It wouldn't work."

"But—"

"We're different people now. In different worlds."

"Cari, what are you saying?"

"Look, for over ten years my life was pathetic. *I* was pathetic. Now for the first time I feel in control and good about the world again. About myself. I have to move on. And I told you I'm seeing someone."

He stared at her in disbelief.

"It's best that we make a clean break. Perhaps we could

get in touch in six months or a year. As friends. Please don't pressure me."

She threw her arms around his neck and kissed him on the cheek.

"Because of those two men? Because of what I did?" When he attempted to embrace her again, she stiffened and held him at arms' length.

"Not only that. Think about it. You committed two murders, but you couldn't commit to me!"

She turned to go. He grabbed her arm.

"You don't even know why I did it."

"Revenge, I suppose. Justice. I can accept all that. Yet—"

"You're wrong! I hated them and wanted to avenge my father, but I had decided against doing any of that until … until …."

She waited for him to continue.

"I realized he would kill again. He as much as told me so. Would probably never stop until someone stopped him." He ran a finger over his scar. "This isn't from a barbed wire fence. Badeen did it with a knife. I'm certain he killed his abusive father. He spent time in prison for another killing years ago. I decided he had to be stopped."

"Good God, Jason!"

"I didn't want you to know, didn't want you to carry the burden of knowing."

She touched his arm. "It would hang over us, would suffuse everything. Every word, every touch, every—"

"You said you had forgiven me."

"I did and I do. But I can't deal with this now, couldn't handle being together, even if you could. I must go. Goodbye, Jason."

She turned and strode down the path they had just followed. He saw in her purposeful gait his father in a coffin, his mother in a cell, Luke in a grave. Before she rounded a curve where the path followed the contour of the lagoon, she glanced back without waving. Then she was gone, and the faint pulse of hope her glance had given him died.

He stood motionless, his eyes fixed on the spot where she

was last visible. She was gone. The wind pierced his jacket. The frigid morning sun shone behind a cloud scrim. He closed his eyes against the stinging, eye-watering cold.

Jason stood like an errant schoolboy across the desk from a grim-faced President Casek.

"No, I won't appoint you on an interim basis," Casek said with heat. "You either take the job or you don't."

"Then I decline. I'll leave the college after spring semester."

"Sounds to me like you're cutting and running. You're not the man for the job after all. Excuse me. I have an important meeting."

Chapter Thirty-Eight

Jason stood before the crucifix in his apartment on a cold, dreary day, his mind somewhere in a wind-swept thicket between thinking and not thinking. He clenched his fists and willed himself to think. His transition to *persona non grata* status at St. Victor College had been subtle but immediate and perceptible.

He was confident that President Casek had said nothing overtly negative about him. The man was too smart and polished for that. In all likelihood, he had merely mentioned to a few well-chosen faculty and administration personnel that Jason, for reasons that he had not seen fit to disclose to the president, had waffled on the position of spiritual director. As a consequence, Casek lacked confidence in appointing Jason to the position.

When Monsignor Korth died eight days following his stroke, Casek appointed a younger priest to the post of spiritual director. The questioning looks, awkward, silence-pocked discussions, and broken-off conversations, all began immediately. After all, Jason had been the heir apparent for several years.

Jason suspected it would only get worse. Now, a month later, his suspicions were daily confirmed. He no longer enjoyed the sense of belonging he had had for nearly ten years on the faculty, a feeling of community that, absent any other family, he cherished.

Which did he regret more, the loss of vocation or of Cari? A toss-up. He hated the self-doubt and self-pity, especially the latter, which he found repulsive. He had the presence of mind to realize he had to push past both and get on with his life, whatever that life might be.

No one other than Monsignor Korth knew of his invalid ordination. Could he convince himself to continue as before with a new assignment at a different Catholic college or university? He had received his PhD in theology, not the most marketable of credentials to offer the secular world.

Since the summer of blood twenty years ago, he had managed to isolate in his psyche what he had done. Therefore, the murders hadn't intruded on his belief system or, in his mind, on the exercise of the orders that flowed from his ordination. Following his confrontation with Monsignor Korth, however, this ingrained habit of compartmentalizing had begun to crack and now had deteriorated into a fracture that continued to compound.

Living a lie had gone beyond discomfort. The lie that enveloped his life assailed him minute by minute. Notwithstanding the fact that he continued to justify the murders he had committed, he had to admit that he could not continue to set rules for the Church. Or, to be more precise, to carve out his own canon within that of the Church.

He could lead his life apart from the Church as he saw fit. If he chose to stay within the Church, he had to do so in conformity with Canon Law. Perhaps the Church wasn't always right, but it always had the right to make the rules.

In order to receive the Holy See's dispensation from a valid ordination, the Canon decreed that a priest had to provide more than a dozen documents in meticulous detail in a strictly prescribed process.

The first step required a letter to the pope with his reasons for leaving the priesthood. This letter would be submitted to the bishop, along with a *curriculum vita* containing in greater detail all the reasons for his defection and why it was irreversible. Forms and statements from others would follow. Interrogations and depositions. Possibly medical testimony.

The Church would scrutinize his original application for admission to Holy Orders and also the documents and affidavits of all those responsible for his admission. The bishop would have to provide an explicit statement of assurance that there would be no scandal if the dispensation were granted. The procedure would take at least a year, possibly longer.

A release from the vow of celibacy formed the root of a high percentage of requests for dispensation. A priest had fallen in love with a woman and felt he could no longer lead a celibate life. Or he had impregnated a woman, which often resulted in the case getting fast-tracked.

Jason recognized the more problematic nature of his situation. Without lying, what reason could he give for wishing to be released from his vows? On the other hand, if he lied to receive dispensation, wouldn't that compound the invalid nature of his ordination and dispensation, and magnify the lie he lived?

If he told the truth, he didn't for a moment doubt that the Church would keep the dispensation proceedings confidential. Given the fact, however, that he would be leaving the priesthood, would the Church direct him to civil authorities? Could they somehow force him to turn himself in without breaking the seal of confidentiality? No.

Besides, the Church would, above all else, choose to avoid scandal, especially one of this magnitude that stemmed from something that had happened two decades before. No, the Church would not direct him anywhere. It would wash its hands of the matter and bounce it back to Jason and his confessor, as it should.

Which pushed him to the fulcrum. Continue as a priest? Out of the question. A personal decision and the right one. As a lay person, following the same reasoning, that of playing by the rules of the Church, he could not participate in the sacraments. Regardless of motive, he was guilty of premeditated murder. So why go through the process of dispensation to become laicized into a state of sacramental limbo?

Why live as a Catholic in name only? He would not confess the murders under any circumstances, which meant he would risk his own salvation. He wasn't sorry for what he had done and never would be, except in the sense that the murders caused him so much vocational stress and turmoil. He shuddered at the shallowness of the thought. To confess would be a lie that would deny his love for Cari and his desire to protect her. In fact, it would be a denial of everything good and decent. So why remain in the all-nourishing fold of the Church at all?

The thought sent a chill through him. Not remain in the Church? Unthinkable. Holy Mother Church was as much a part of him as his lungs or his brain. Yet, what other conclusion made sense? The Church was part of him, but he wasn't part of the Church. An image of a naked man adrift on an ice floe flitted across his mind.

He would not make a decision today. He had much to consider.

Chapter Thirty-Nine

Current vocational angst aside, he had to figure out how to make a living. Going to another Catholic school as a lay teacher or counselor did not appeal to him. The past would always follow him, either during the vetting process or later. He could never outrun or evade his history in the small universe of Catholic academia. *You were a priest? What happened? Did you receive dispensation? You didn't? What exactly happened?*

These questions and dozens more would create in some minds an initial aura of mystery that would quickly morph into dark suspicion and distrust. Worse than the questions asked would be the unasked ones, to say nothing of the whispers and looks and sidelong glances.

Calls would be made, emails sent. The suspicions triggered by the absence of a formal dispensation would make him the same kind of pariah that he was becoming at St. Victor.

The dregs of winter settled in. The day following the final varsity basketball game, Dan Petrakis showed up at Jason's apartment.

"Bring me up to date, Mr. Petrakis."

"Sure thing, Father. Our last conversation really got me thinking. Rachel—that's my girlfriend—and I had some real heart-to-hearts, and we've decided, well, a couple of things. She's going to put the baby up for adoption and, ah, we aren't together anymore."

"You realized you would face the same kinds of issues again."

"You got it. Took a lot of tears and screaming and, yeah, sex. We finally decided we should make a clean break while

195

we're young. Once we agreed on that, we got our folks involved. Man oh man, fireworks all over the place at first, especially from her old man. We hung in there and worked it all out. I learned a lot about myself. I feel great."

"I'm happy for you, Dan. You're ending your college years on a high note and charging into the world with less weight on your shoulders."

"Thanks, Father. The tough part is making a decision. After that, it's full steam ahead, you know?"

Jason smiled and led him to the door. "Always look ahead. Remember, it's what you do with the future that counts."

"Father, when are you hearing confessions again? I haven't gone yet."

"I'm scheduled for the box this Saturday at four. Saint Victor Chapel. Better bring lunch. I might keep you awhile."

Dan laughed as he stepped through the doorway. "Sure thing, Father."

Receive the Holy Spirit; whose sins you shall forgive, they are forgiven them; and whose sins you shall retain, they are retained.

Was this now true in his case? Had it ever been true?

Jason peered out his window. Students streamed in and out of St. Victor Hall and up the hill toward Duquesne Hall and the center of campus. He glanced at his watch. Five minutes to four. Many of the students had finished classes for the day; others scurried to their final one. As he watched, the sun slanted in from the southwest to brighten those sections of landscape not blocked by buildings and trees. Remaining patches of snow gleamed against the dark, wet earth.

He had two hours before dinner in the faculty dining room. He didn't feel like correcting the student term papers on his desk, or preparing a presentation to the pre-seminarians at a dinner scheduled next week.

He took his father's bugle from the crucifix and dropped into his easy chair. He seldom watched television, but now he flicked on the remote and absent-mindedly surfed the channels. He came to someone interviewing an actor whose face he recognized, though he couldn't think of the man's name.

"You've played so many widely differing roles," the interviewer said, *"romantic leading man, mob assassin, suburban father of six—the list goes on. No typecasting for you. How do you do that without losing your credibility or fan base, one of the staunchest in the history of Hollywood?"*

"Let's be honest. Luck has played a big role. Part of that luck is my ability to be what I'm not for a short period. That is, long enough to make a picture. Nothing unusual there. Except for that bit of good fortune, I can't be what I'm not, and that's my secret: I know who I am. My wife of thirty years can confirm that. Any time I forget, all it takes is a look from her to remind me." He laughed. *"Another part of my good luck—my wife."*

The actor, effectively self-effacing, came across as a good guy. He had said nothing out of the ordinary, yet what he said struck Jason as elemental and profound: the man knew himself. Jason turned off the TV.

He would commence the next chapter of his life without going through the ordeal of a formal dispensation. According to Canon Law, he had received his vocation invalidly. *Ergo*, he was not a priest and would vacate his chosen vocation pre-emptively. He would remain on St. Victor's payroll for a few more months before striking out on his own.

Closing his eyes, he said a Hail Mary before turning to the crucifix and hanging the bugle back on the nail. He knelt and kissed the foot of Christ. Then he crossed over to his desk, tapped his computer, and raised the Internet.

Full steam ahead, Mr. Petrakis.

For the next two months Jason carried on with his daily routine: celebrant at mass each morning at six, classroom instruction, committee meetings, confessions, meals in the faculty dining room.

Meanwhile, his quest for a suitable occupation simmered in his mind constantly. He had a universe of choices. Well, yes and no. Early on he ruled out business, which struck him as

197

sterile, too money-oriented, and foreign to his temperament.

He considered missionary work, the Peace Corps, even law enforcement. Nothing clicked. He wanted to teach and counsel, preferably in a religious environment. But where? And what about the inevitable background checks?

He briefly considered the order of St. Benedict and also the Christian Brothers, concluding that they would raise even more questions than a college or university would and likely not accept him. If they did, he would face the same issues that would surface at any other Catholic religious institution.

He had no desire for the time being to join a non-Catholic one because he would feel like an outsider, though he suspected this would change over time.

His last paycheck would arrive June first. He had to vacate his apartment by the end of June. Graduation approached, and he still found himself unable to determine a course of action.

On a Monday morning late in May, while waiting his turn with the oral hygienist, he flipped through the pages of a magazine. An article on teaching in prison caught his eye. Actually, the byline caught his attention. It said simply, "Brother Timothy."

The hygienist called him in just as he began reading the piece, so he took the three-month-old magazine with him. The hygienist, a pretty redhead he had not seen on previous visits, was well organized and began as soon as he sat in the chair.

"Busy day?" he asked, to make conversation.

"You said it. The other hygienist called in sick. We're trying to take care of as many patients as we can. Here, hold this. You might want to take a look later." She handed him a large mirror and got to work.

When she finished, she smiled sweetly—he guessed her age at twenty-two or -three—and handed him a new Oral-B toothbrush and floss sample. "You're good to go!"

He thanked her and proceeded to the front desk. A minute later a matronly woman gazed at her computer monitor and said, "November 20, Father. Morning or afternoon?"

"Let me get back to you on that, Carol. Things are a little fluid right now for next fall. By the way, could you make me a copy of this article?"

"Of course."

She rose from her chair and took the magazine. Glancing at it, she paused. "Why, this is from February. Just take it with you."

He didn't leave the parking lot until he had skimmed the article by Brother Timothy, who led a group called Brothers of the 11th Hour. Their motto appeared at the end of the article: "Knowledge Is Freedom." The article dealt at some length with what the Brothers did—teaching exclusively in a prison environment—but revealed little about the organization itself.

The anecdotes about teaching in prison ranged from funny to sad to tragic among a population that represented a composite of the dark side of the human condition. Many of the inmates were the worst remnants of society and beyond redemption, including many lifers. What good would any learning do them? And who would want to spend his days with the likes of the Badeens and Sinkhorns of the world? Better to let them rot in ignorance.

He threw the magazine into a trash container at the Exxon station when he filled his tank. Upon reaching his apartment, he had second thoughts and conducted an Internet search for the organization. He found a website that provided scant information. However, it had a 'Contact Us' button.

The Brothers of the 11th Hour operated in Landover, a city of 13,000 that nestled on a strip of earth between the Wisconsin and Fox rivers in south-central Wisconsin. The Chamber of Commerce called it the "Gateway to the North." The Fox River flowed north to the St. Lawrence, while the Wisconsin River flowed southwest to the Mississippi. The town had developed commercially because everyone from trappers to missionaries had had to portage their canoes and other craft across the neck of land between the two rivers.

The state had opened the Two Rivers Correctional Facility in Landover in 1991. Comprising ninety-five acres, it had an original inmate capacity of five hundred. The average daily prisoner population in recent years had nearly doubled that number. He decided to pay a visit to the Brothers of the 11th Hour.

Jason called Brother Timothy first, refrained from asking for information, and pointedly cut Brother Timothy off when he seemed about to volunteer any. He wanted to meet the man in person, on his turf, without any preconceived notions.

Brother Timothy's physique appeared to have progressed from adolescent chubbiness to middle-age spread. His shock of blond hair graced him with an air of boyishness. Not knowing what to expect, Jason had worn civvies for the interview.

They exchanged pleasantries for a few moments. Brother Timothy offered Jason coffee and he accepted.

After pouring the coffee, Brother Timothy slung himself into a swivel chair behind a scarred and worn steel desk. "So what do you want to know?"

"Tell me exactly what you do."

"Okay, here goes. The good, the bad, and the ugly. We have nine people. We all live in this converted brewery in little two-room apartments. We eat most meals in our community dining room, such as it is. Anyone can live on his own if he has the means—off campus, as it were. We are secular.

"We each receive a small salary for teaching five days a week at Two Rivers. What do we teach? Basic reading, writing, and arithmetic. A lot of first and second grade stuff. An amazingly high percentage of inmates are very smart, some with IQs that go off the chart. But they can't read or write. Why? Many are dyslexic. Some were completely unmotivated and/or abused during their formative years. Others bounced from place to place or lived in a car with a parent, usually the mother, and never stayed in school long enough to learn anything before turning to crime.

"We try to equip them with the rudiments and give them some confidence. If they do get back to the outside, they might have a chance to make it. If they never get out, they'll at least have the ability to use their minds to read and broaden their world. The drudgery quotient is as high for the teacher as the frustration level is for most of his students."

"What kind of person do you look for? What kind of credentials?"

Brother Timothy leaned forward and grabbed a handful of M&Ms from a glass bowl on his desk. "Help yourself," he said. Jason scooped up a handful.

"Most of us burned out in some other line of work. Some of us spent time in jail once or twice. All of us are probably running from something—a spouse, bounty hunter, ourselves, God. Who knows?"

Jason shifted in his chair. "Sounds like a tough, motley bunch. How do you check them out?"

"I don't. I go on instinct. If the law turns up and snaps the cuffs on one of us, which has happened once in eight years, well, we try to replace him. We're teaching murderers and rapists at no charge. What's anyone going to do to us?"

He popped a few M&Ms into his mouth.

"We teach and we try to raise enough money to keep food on the table and pay the rent. All of us raise money by calling people, companies, and foundations to ask for donations. Some of us give lectures and ask for money.

"Each of us keeps twenty percent of the money we individually raise. We've managed to stay ahead of our bills for the past six years. I rounded up the original seed money for the first two years."

"What do you want to know about me?"

"Nothing. If I ever find out you're wanted for anything more than a misdemeanor, we'll have a come-to-Jesus talk, and you'd better come clean with me. I call the police on killers, pedophiles, and rapists. Other stuff gets handled case by case. If you fall into one of those categories, I suggest you leave right now.

"The state allows us to go on its property and do our thing, and I have certain understandings with the warden that I won't violate. We try to light a candle or two. We don't want a conflagration."

Although fully aware of the irony of leaving one lie to

enter another, Jason decided on the spot he would not admit his murders to Brother Timothy.

Full steam ahead, Mr. Petrakis.

He had found a new home, at least for the time being. Other matters populated his new world, one in particular: Celibacy. *Celibacy.* Thirty-five years old and probably one of the few people in the world who had experienced sex only once. There were undoubtedly more men who had never had sex than there were who had had it once, for having it one time would dictate having it again and again. Only through a herculean commitment and continuing effort could a man abstain after once having experienced it. He was one of those men.

Carnal thoughts of women always lurked at the edges and often intruded boldly to the point of rude discomfort, no matter the hour or place.

In seminary a fellow seminarian had once asked the spiritual director, an eighty-three-year-old priest, when lustful thoughts ceased. Jason was convinced at the time that the question was on the mind of every seminarian in the room. The old priest, Father McMahon, had held the seminarian in a gaze of mock sternness and said, with a certain twinkle in his eye, "When it happens, I'll let you know." Relieved laughter had filled the room.

Remaining celibate involved strict avoidance daily of any situation that could lead to temptation stronger than what existed in thought. As often as Jason had to confess his carnal thoughts to his confessor, he never confessed those about Cari. His confessions of lust always remained generic. To name her or even to identify her as someone from his childhood, would have been tantamount to a betrayal, a violation of Cari and of a sacred act that had occurred during a time of innocence, an act that had given him the strength to withstand the onslaught on his soul following the murders he had committed.

Except for Cari, the deep knowledge of evil that had marked his childhood may well have destroyed his ability to lead a productive, positive life. She had kept him from suffering one of the worst human defeats conceivable, that of failing to become what one is capable of becoming. His refusal to confess may have stemmed from a flawed pride, but in equal measure he felt proud of Cari and her impact on his life.

A duality characterized his attitude toward sex. A certain fear counteracted the ever-present desire. He knew that his female students, their mothers, and other women found him attractive. Not that he deceived himself. Part of the attraction lay in his collar, which made him, at least theoretically, unattainable. The excitement of forbidden fruit intensified the mystery and at the same time created a margin of safety for immature and mature women alike. The scar on his forehead implied danger and created curiosity to add to the mystery.

Of course, he had virtually no intimate social experience with women. How would he bridge that void? Any thought of the bar scene was as foreign to him as the Milky Way. Singles groups? He cringed.

He marveled at and loved the infinite physical and temperamental variety of women. He appreciated their beauty, their mannerisms, the essence of their femininity—all of which constituted and exacerbated part of his fear.

Should he forsake his lifelong celibacy, he sensed that he ran the risk of falling hard for the first woman he slept with, only to live to regret it later, or becoming a complete libertine—a little kid with five dollars in a candy store. He winced at his sophomoric metaphor.

Through ordination, prayer, and the execution of pastoral duties, priests were to experience the sublimation of their sexual nature. Jason couldn't speak for others, but this had not occurred for him, at least not to the degree he had hoped it would. His concupiscence had never quieted.

As a young priest, he had read something by the Greek philosopher Epicurus. The passage had struck him so strongly that he had typed it and put it into his wallet, one of two quotations he kept there. He extracted them both.

It is not the young man who should be considered

203

fortunate, but the old man who has lived well, because the young man in his prime wanders much by chance, vacillating in his beliefs, while the old man has docked in the harbor, having safeguarded his true happiness.

He still wanted to believe the thought. However, he was neither young nor old, nor was he at all sure of his beliefs. Far from being docked in harbor, he found himself adrift in a seething sea.

The other quotation he had always lived by was of a more modern vintage from President Calvin Coolidge.

Nothing in the world can take the place of Persistence. Talent will not; nothing is more common than unsuccessful men with talent. Genius will not; unrewarded genius is almost a proverb. Education will not; the world is full of educated derelicts. Persistence and determination alone are omnipotent. The slogan Press On has solved and always will solve the problems of the human race.

But at what would he persist? What did he want to become? For the time being he would live in the converted brewery with the Brothers of the 11th Hour and would remain celibate.

Although cut off from the sacraments, he would attend mass every Sunday and sometimes during the week. Perhaps the passage of time would provide answers that would lead to reconciliation with the church he loved. He could not deal with that potentiality at the present. One right-angle turn in his life would have to suffice for now.

Chapter Forty

2012

His last session of the day having ended, Jason told the guard he needed a few minutes to take some notes and wrap things up, which wasn't true. That morning he had read an email six times before printing it. Now he wanted time to read it again before his ride arrived.

Hi Jason,

Thanks for replying to my email. So nice to hear from you after so many years. Will write more later, but in a few minutes I'm leaving for a jazz weekend in Kansas City with my friend Rhonda, who plays in the symphony with me. (Guess you could say we're slumming; we're both having a fling with our new love, jazz.)

The guy I told you about when your mother died wasn't so sweet after all. He left my life shortly after you did. Utter devastation for a while, but know what? I've really acclimated to the single state and believe I'll stay that way. One problem: I'm not programmed for celibacy. No way. (What's a girl to do?) Speaking of which, did you hear that Father Ed and a certain Sister Alphonsa from Augustine High hooked up and took off? Quite a long time ago, actually. Never heard of the nun. I recalled the priest's name and how fond you were of him. Guess you're not the only kinky priest to go AWOL.

Must admit, though, it surprised me to hear you had left the priesthood. Never thought you would, but I'm happy you have found fulfillment in your prison ministry (right word?) as a brother of some sort. You weren't altogether clear on any of that. Anyway, so glad I found you. Isn't the Internet a miracle? Let's keep in touch. Love you and miss you.

Cari

The words of "Somewhere My Love" echoed in his mind along with the haunting sound of Cari's violin, when the notes had flown through the darkness of those sacred nights from her bedroom so long ago.

Somewhere, my love, there will be songs to sing
Although the snow covers the hopes of spring
Somewhere a hill blossoms in green and gold
And there are dreams, all that your heart can hold
Someday we'll meet again, my love
Someday whenever the spring breaks through

You'll come to me out of the long-ago
Warm as the wind, soft as the kiss of snow
Till then, my sweet, think of me now and then
Godspeed, my love, till you are mine again!

He folded the sheet of paper and slid it into the breast pocket of his threadbare navy sport coat. Melancholy laced the thrill of hearing from Cari. He missed her as much as he missed the diminished role of the Church in his life. He thought of Luke, who had gone to his grave half, not whole. Would he himself end up the same way emotionally?

Love you and miss you!

He knocked on the door to signal the guard. A few

checkpoints later, he reached the outside. Right on time as usual, Brother Timothy rolled up in his rattletrap Ford station wagon.

"Did you qualify anyone for parole?" Timothy asked.

"Not a one. I have more lifers than Alcatraz ever did. Who the devil called a meeting for four o'clock on Friday?"

"I did. It'll be short. Then we'll have a beer. Or two or three. Better tend to your lapel pin."

Jason looked down to see the violin medallion from Cari hanging by a thread on the lapel of his jacket right next to a small brass crucifix. He refastened the clasp and allowed his fingers to linger on the medallion.

"You big on music? I never see you listening to it. You ever play that old bugle you have in your room?"

Jason gazed through the windshield for a few moments before answering.

"My bugle repertoire consists of one piece of music." He ran his index finger over the medallion. "The violin is the most sublime musical instrument ever invented. For me it brings to mind beauty and love and a longing for wholeness I'll probably never experience in this life. Yeah, you could say I'm a music fan."

The weathered old buildings surrounding the long-defunct brewery that served as their headquarters had seen better days. Renovation had begun on some of them. The old brewery, however, had not yet met the word renovation, let alone become acquainted with it.

Inside, amid a faint odor of malt, they wended their way between army-green desks and filing cabinets to a conference room at the back. Brother Tim glanced at his watch. "They're probably waiting for us. We're a few minutes late."

"Serve you right if no one showed up, Timothy. I'm of a notion to cut out myself. For God's sake, couldn't your meeting wait till Monday?"

Brother Tim laughed and opened the door for him. A dozen people packed the small room. A collective shout rang out: 'Happy Anniversary, Jason!'"

A large makeshift sign in red proclaimed, HAPPY 5th.

207

Balloons and crepe paper streamers filled the room. A cake, a box of wine, and a cooler of beer awaited them.

"Speech! Speech!" Brother Tim said, and the others all took up the mantra. Jason raised his hand to quiet them.

"Well, you got me. Thank you so much. I can say without reservation that the last five years have been happy and rewarding. I haven't felt such contentment since before my father died when I was fourteen. You are truly my family. Now, will someone please give me a beer before I get totally maudlin?"

A roar of affirmation filled the air as several people surrounded the cooler and others pressed forward to shake his hand. Someone handed him a can of beer. Although happy in the merriment of the moment, he wasn't really in the moment. His thoughts journeyed to an undefined faraway place as he caressed the violin medallion on his lapel.

APPENDIX
Questions for discussion groups.

1. Is vigilante justice ever justified? Discuss.

2. Does moral law supersede statutory law? Put another way, how do we resolve conflicts between personal morality and church and/or state laws? Who decides? Can you provide an example, pro or con?

3. Regarding vigilante justice, how does real life differ from fiction?

3. Do we act according to our beliefs, or do we end up believing as we act? Is this another way of saying we rationalize our actions if in the beginning they violate our belief system?

4. In Catholic theology and at least some Protestant faiths, God requires repentance ("repent or perish") as a prerequisite for forgiveness. On the other hand, we are told to forgive those who injure us, even if they don't show remorse or ask our forgiveness ("turn the other cheek"). Does this mean human beings are held to a higher standard than God in this respect? How do you see this idea implemented, or not, in day-to-day life?

5. What exactly does it mean to love your enemies? Is this a reasonable concept?

6. What are your feelings toward Jason? Do you like him? Why or why not? Do you feel empathy for him?

7. What are your reactions to Cari? Do you like her? Why or why not? Do you feel empathy for her?

8. Should Jason have continued on as a priest? Or did he do the right thing to walk away from his vows in the manner he did?

9. Do you think Jason and Cari will get back together? Would it work out if they did?

10. Should Jason have told Cari specifically why he killed the two men? Should he ever tell her?

11. Jason tells Monsignor Korth that God either made Badeen and Sinkhorn the way they were or He gave them free will and they chose to do evil. Then he says he did the responsible thing to protect Cari and maybe others from two men who in all likelihood would have killed again. If science were ever to show convincingly that in a legal sense people do not have free will, what impact would such a finding have on our criminal justice system? That is, what would we do with criminals?

12. What would you do if faced with Jason's decision, protect Cari in the only way he saw possible or abide by the conventional morality he had been taught?

    Would you have the courage to overcome your fear of failing and of the strong probability of losing your life?

    What if you were certain you would not fail and would not be found out by the authorities?

13. Other issues for discussion?

About the Author

Peter Shianna has written two previous novels, *Love Tag* and *Take Off*, both published by traditional small presses. *Love Tag* won the 2010 Royal Palm Literary Award for mainstream fiction. Other award-winning work has appeared in the Rockhurst Review, the Kansas City Star, and the Creative Writer's Notebook Journeys Anthology Series, as well as several other anthologies. A licensed private pilot, Peter loves golf and pickleball. He and his wife Lori live in Florida.